THE SPOOKOSCOPE

CECI JENKINSON

Illustrations by

Michael Broad

ff

faber and faber

First published in 2009
by Faber and Faber Limited
Bloomsbury House, 74–77 Great Russell Street,
London WC1B 3DA

Designed by Mandy Norman
Printed in England by CPI Bookmarque, Croydon

A CIP record for this book
is available from the British Library

ISBN 978–0–571–24074–6

2 4 6 8 10 9 7 5 3 1

For Susie and K – quite simply the best

CONTENTS

The ghostly white figure moved slowly across the gallery, watched by a wide-eyed crowd in the Great Hall below. Pausing by a heavy curtain, the spectre gave a chilling moan – and vanished. The spellbound watchers gasped – none would ever forget the Ghost of Spiffing Castle.

When Lady Spiffing had waved goodbye to the last of the visitors, she went up to the small room behind the gallery, where the ghost was now sitting in an old chair.

'How was I?' asked the ghost.

'Not bad,' she replied. 'I wasn't sure about the moan, though. It was a bit dramatic.'

The ghost pulled his sheet off to reveal Lord Spiffing underneath, old and bony but very much alive. 'I wanted to vary my act a bit,' he sighed. 'I'm getting rather tired of haunting.'

'Oh, but you're so good at it. Pass me that sheet to fold up. It's getting all crushed. Ghosts don't have crushed sheets. And think of all the tourists who come to see you. Today it was twenty-three – that's a record.'

'We need every penny,' said Lord Spiffing. 'This morning I had to put out yet another bucket to catch the rain in King George's Bedroom.'

'It's a good thing King George doesn't sleep there these days, then,' remarked Lady Spiffing.

'Quite soon the whole roof will come down,' sighed her husband.

'Then we'll just need one very big bucket.'

'It's serious, Binky. It might even be time for Drastic Measures.'

Lady Spiffing frowned. Drastic Measures meant selling the dogs or her husband's beloved Jersey cow, Mildred. Whenever the conversation turned to Drastic Measures, Lord Spiffing was inclined to become very gloomy.

'Cheer up,' she said. 'I think I might have the answer. Look at this.' From the pocket of her skirt she produced a small advertisement cut from a newspaper:

Madam Violet Moonbeam
Clairvoyant Extraordinaire!

Do you require communication with your Dear Departed?

I can unlock the secrets of the spirit world and bring peace of mind!

Lord Spiffing looked at the advertisement doubtfully.

'It's not peace of mind we need, it's money,' he pointed out. 'In any case, I certainly don't require communication with *any* of my departed, dear or otherwise.'

'I know you don't, but this Moonbeam woman might be able to rally up a few of our ghosts. We both know they are floating about all over the place – if they would only show themselves to the tourists, you wouldn't have to get under that sheet three times a week.'

'Ah-ha. When you put it like that, my dear,' said Lord Spiffing, 'I agree.'

So a letter was sent that very day to Madam Violet Moonbeam, inviting her to come and rally up the Spiffing ancestors.

By a spooky coincidence, Oli Biggles and his best friend Skipjack Haynes, who both lived less than a mile away from Spiffing Castle, were also talking about ghosts. Skipjack's big brother Matt had just arrived home for his college holidays and the boys were helping him carry his stuff upstairs when Skipjack spotted something strange stuffed into an overflowing cardboard box.

'What's this?' he asked, pulling out a red

contraption covered with rubber suckers and trailing wire tentacles. 'It looks like a remote-control jellyfish.'

'Careful,' said Matt. 'It's a ghost detector.'

'You're kidding! Where did you get it?' Oli asked.

'I made it. It's part of my course.'

'I thought engineering was about building bridges, not ghost detectors,' said Skipjack.

'Oh, I gave up engineering – too much like hard work,' replied Matt. 'I switched to para-psychology.'

'Para-whatty?'

'Para-psychology. The study of ghosts. But I haven't told Mum and Dad yet, so keep it quiet, OK?'

'Have you seen any ghosts yet?' asked Oli.

'No.' Matt frowned. 'I need to perfect my ghost detector.'

Skipjack looked at the ghost detector more carefully and spotted its secret. 'It's a scrum cap with goggles!'

'Clever, huh?' said Matt. 'I got the idea playing rugby. I needed something close-fitting for the sensors to work. First I tried a swimming cap, but that just looked stupid.'

Skipjack pulled on the scrum cap and shook his head so that the wires bounced about like antennae on an alien's helmet. 'And this doesn't look stupid?' he enquired.

'On you it does,' said Matt. 'On me it looks scientifically brilliant.'

'How does it work?' asked Oli.

'Well, the theory is that ghosts are basically centres of electro-magnetic activity,' began Matt. 'We'd all be able to see them if we were tuned in. These discs are electrodes – sensors which magnify the electro-magnetic activity so that the brain can detect it.'

Skipjack's eyes were beginning to glaze over at these technical details but Matt was on a roll. He held up a black box the size of a pack of cards, which was attached to the scrum cap by a long wire. 'This control box measures the change of magnetic flux in frequency cycles per second and the wavelengths of e-m radiations – it's basically like a spectroscope –'

'Argh!' wailed Skipjack. Clapping his hands

over his ears, he screwed his eyes shut and began to shout, 'Bibble-bibble-bibble-bibble-bibble!'
Matt stared.

'Too much science,' explained Oli. 'It's like an allergic reaction. You can only talk about science for about thirty seconds before he starts bibbling like this. He can't help it – he does it at school, too. It gets him into loads of trouble. Tell me about the goggles.'

'They've got special lenses,' Matt said, still with one eye on Skipjack, 'Which are sensitive to ghosts. It's all very scientific. I don't know why I can't get it to work.'

'Has he finished?' yelled Skipjack.

'Yes!' shouted Oli.

Skipjack uncovered his ears. 'At last. I wish we could take your Spookoscope on our school history trip on Thursday. We're going to Spiffing Castle, which is stuffed with ghosts.'

'Well, you can't,' his brother told him. 'I forbid you on pain of a Fate Worse Than Death.'

Oli was examining the control box. 'What are these buttons for?' he asked.

'That's the on/off switch,' explained Matt, pointing. 'And see that dial? That's the electro-magnetic activity meter. It can go from zero to sixty in 4.3 seconds.'

'Awesome,' said Oli. 'Like a Ferrari. And this?' He pointed to a red button which could be turned to low, medium or high.

'Whatever happens, *don't* touch that,' Matt told him.

Skipjack immediately longed to touch it. 'Why

not?' he asked. 'What does it do?'

'It's the Psychic Surge button,' said his brother. 'It could do anything.'

A pink flush spread over the powdered face of Madam Violet Moonbeam as she sat in her tiny lounge and read the Spiffings' letter. A Lord and Lady! In a castle! Such grandness!

She wondered if she would need to curtsey. During all her years as an actress in the theatre, Violet Moonbeam had done a thousand curtseys. Now that she was too old to look beautiful, and too proud to look old, the stage had lost its sparkle. But the rent still had to be paid, so it was lucky that during those years she had learned all about theatrical special effects. Violet Moonbeam decided to mix stage acting with stage trickery to sell herself as someone who

…ld contact the spirit world – a clairvoyant.

Of course, Violet Moonbeam could no more talk to ghosts than fly a spaceship, but she could *act* as if she could and her customers would never know the difference. Indeed she had been such a hit so far that she almost believed in her own performances.

'I *am* a clairvoyant extraordinaire,' she told herself happily, and went to pack.

Lord Spiffing was in the sunny meadow below the castle talking to his Jersey cow Mildred when the station taxi passed by. He frowned: the sign on the gates clearly said 'Closed on Tuesdays'.

Couldn't people read nowadays?

Violet Moonbeam noticed the old herdsman with his gentle cow as her cab trundled up the drive. When the castle loomed ahead, tall and thin and pointy, she sat back in her seat with a sigh. Such grandness!

The taxi brought her to a magnificent wooden front door and the driver heaved her two coffin-sized suitcases out of the boot before taking his payment and driving away. Violet Moonbeam pulled a big iron ring marked BELL and waited to meet her first real live butler.

Presently she heard a voice calling, 'Hello?'

She looked around and was surprised to see a

woman's head poking out of a downstairs window.

'Hello,' said the head again. 'You must be Madam Moonbeam. I'm Agatha Spiffing. Would you mind coming in this way? I'm afraid the front door is completely rotten, so we daren't use it in case it falls off its hinges completely. And now we've lost the key to the garden door, the one the visitors normally use. You could go round to the back door, but it's rather a long walk. Here's a stepladder.'

Violet Moonbeam watched with displeasure as this apparatus came clattering through the window. She was an actress, not an acrobat.

'We can fetch your suitcases later,' said her hostess, 'with the wheelbarrow. Our caretaker, Wilson, used to do odd jobs like that before he got too old. Now we must do everything ourselves.'

Violet Moonbeam had prepared a dramatic entrance into Spiffing Castle, in which she would sweep into a hall sprinkled with footmen, and be so overwhelmed by ghostly presences that she would have to lie on a velvet couch to recover.

Possibly she would be fanned by the footmen. Everyone would be impressed by her psychic sensitivity.

Clambering up a stepladder into a clutter of hats and boots and dog beds made it a little trickier to create such a spiritual effect. But Violet Moonbeam was a true professional and could always summon up a performance, even in a cloakroom.

'Lady Spiffing,' she panted as she hauled her

second sturdy leg in through the window and planted it on the floor. 'Already here I can sense the spirits that roam the castle, sad and restless.'

'How marvellous,' replied her hostess. 'I can only sense mud and dogs. You must be very gifted. Come and have some tea and we'll tell you what we need.'

Violet Moonbeam kept up her hopes of grandness all the way along the damp and cobwebby passage to a kitchen the size of a sports hall. But where was the cook? Where were all the maids? Why was Lady Spiffing herself putting the kettle on to boil?

As she stood by the window wondering and watching the chickens pecking in the weedy yard, she spotted the scruffy old cow-man again in one of the crumbling sheds. He was peering into corners and reaching out now and then to pluck something invisible out of the air. What *was* he up to?

'Here we are,' said her hostess, setting an old, chipped teapot on the table.

The kitchen door creaked open and in pottered the old cow-man.

'I've got some more cobwebs,' he announced.

'Well done, dear,' said Lady Spiffing. 'We'll hang them up later. Come and meet Madam Moonbeam. She had to climb in through the cloakroom window because I couldn't find the key to the garden door.'

'Ah-ha. In my pocket, I'm afraid.'

Lady Spiffing sighed. 'Madam Moonbeam, this is my husband, Algernon.'

'Husband?' squawked Violet Moonbeam and then coughed. Lord Spiffing had come to shake her hand and she was overwhelmed by a powerful smell of cow.

'Delighted,' he beamed. He was a tall man, apparently too tall for his hair, which had retreated from the summit of his head to grow in woolly tufts over his ears. 'I thought you were just a nincompoop of a tourist when you drove past but Mildred – that's my cow – put me right by wagging her tail. She's amazing, you know. I'm convinced she has psychic powers of her own. You must come and meet her one day, Madam Moonbeam – you'd have a lot in common. Now, do take a seat and we'll give you the low-down, as they say.'

By the time Lord and Lady Spiffing had finished, Violet Moonbeam realised that there would be no butler or cook, no footmen or maids. Just two old people trying to find enough money to stop their home falling down. She considered owning up that she wasn't really a clairvoyant, but she changed her mind. They might send her away again, and they weren't the only ones who needed cash.

So she asked, 'Where would you like the first ghost to appear?'

'Well, the Great Hall is always a popular place for sightings,' suggested Lord Spiffing.

'Then that is where I shall encourage the spirits of your Dear Departed to communicate with you,' declared Madam Moonbeam.

His Lordship shifted uncomfortably. 'Ah-ha. Do I have to be communicated with? My departed were not very dear.'

But Violet Moonbeam was not to be denied the chance of performing her Dear Departed scene in such splendid surroundings. 'As their Loved One Still With Us, you must be present,' she insisted. 'We will meet in the Great Hall at seven this evening. I shall need to be alone there for two hours beforehand, to prepare myself spiritually.'

'While you do that,' said Lady Spiffing, 'we'll bring those cobwebs in, before they blow away.'

'I am just a teensy bit curious about why you collect cobwebs, Lady Spiffing?'

'To decorate the castle of course. Tourists love cobwebs. We found out quite by accident, when we got behind with the cleaning. It's very convenient.'

'I see,' said Violet Moonbeam, doubtfully. 'I shall now prepare to meet your Dear Departed,' and she blew out of the room in a cloud of purple.

'I do wish she wouldn't keep calling them that,' sighed Lord Spiffing.

At seven o'clock precisely, Lord and Lady Spiffing knocked on the door of the Great Hall.

'Just a minute,' called Madam Moonbeam. She made a final check of her preparations. The curtains were drawn and the hidden mini-projector correctly positioned. She had placed the small table and three chairs near a big portrait of an ugly ancestor. A thread tied to a crystal chandelier ran down behind the ugly ancestor and across the floor to the leg of the chair that she would sit in. She double-checked the name on the ugly ancestor's gilded frame: Gerald. She sat down at the table.

'Come in!' she called.

When Lord and Lady Spiffing were safely seated in the semi-darkness, Madam Moonbeam put her fingertips together, closed her eyes and called, ‘Is there a Spirit there?’

Lord Spiffing was seized by a terrible urge to giggle and he made a strange snorting sound which was silenced by a wifely kick in the shins beneath the table.

‘I can feel your presence, Spirit,’ cooed Madam Moonbeam. ‘Give us a sign.’ She shifted in her seat until her left foot found the thread tied to her chair leg.

The chandelier tinkled.

‘Well, I’m jiggered!’ cried Lord Spiffing. ‘Ask who it is.’

‘Who are you?’ hooted Madam Moonbeam.

The chandelier tinkled again.

‘I’m hearing a name beginning with G . . .’ whispered Madam Moonbeam. ‘Could it be – Gerald?’

‘Good grief!’ exclaimed Lord Spiffing. ‘Gerald was my great-great-grandfather. That’s his portrait, right behind you.’

‘Do you have a message, Gerald?’ called Madam Moonbeam.

There was a long tinkle in response.

‘Gerald says he wants to help you,’ translated

Madam Moonbeam. 'He promises to appear whenever you have tourists in the Great Hall. He says he will give you a demonstration now.'

She pressed a small remote control in her lap and on the gallery, exactly where Lord Spiffing had paraded in his sheet, appeared a white, shimmering figure.

'It's Gerald!' breathed Lord Spiffing. 'He's a lot thinner than in his portrait.'

'He probably doesn't eat much these days,' his wife pointed out.

The figure flickered and disappeared.

Lord Spiffing turned to congratulate Madam Moonbeam, but she had slumped back in her chair with her eyes closed, exhausted by the strain of rallying up Gerald.

'Shh,' whispered Lady Spiffing. 'Let her sleep.'

They crept out together.

Oli and his sister Tara usually cycled past Skipjack's house to collect him on the way to school. Tara was a year younger than Oli, with a snub nose and dark hair that was always escaping from whatever it had been tied in. She was fiercely independent and although she would, occasionally, unite with her brother against a common enemy, their alliances were usually brief and always uneasy.

On this Thursday morning, as usual, Skipjack was propped against the gatepost on his bike. Usually on a Thursday morning Oli's friend had the desperate look of a Bibbler who would have to endure double science before break. But this was the morning of the Spiffing Castle History Trip, and Skipjack's freckled face bore a grin that stretched from one ear to the other.

'Guess what I've got in my backpack?' he asked Oli.

'A rugby ball?'

'Well, of course. But that's not what I meant. Guess again.'

'A triple pepperoni pizza?'

'Oh, rats. I knew I'd forgotten something. Never mind. It's the Spookoscope, Oli – I've got the Spookoscope!'

'What about Matt?' asked Oli, 'And the Fate Worse Than Death?'

'Matt's gone away till Sunday night,' beamed

Skipjack, 'So we're fate-free till then.'

Oli grinned. 'Bags go first.'

Skipjack held up a hand like a policeman stopping traffic. 'Not so fast, matey. I am related to this Spookoscope by blood. I'm going first.'

'What is a spookoscope, anyway?' Tara wanted to know.

'It's a machine that detects ghosts,' explained Oli.

'I don't believe in ghosts,' announced his sister. 'If ghosts really existed someone would have proved it by now. Daisy says all so-called ghosts are just tricks.'

Daisy Levity was Tara's best friend. She was also a recognised expert on tricks, being the granddaughter of Doctor Hamish Levity who ran the joke shop where Skipjack spent all his pocket money.

'We might find things with the Spookoscope,' suggested Oli, 'that even Daisy can't explain.'

'Rubbish,' said Tara.

The school trip was for Tara and Daisy's year as well as Oli and Skipjack's, all under the eagle eye of Miss Harridan, Head of History. Miss Harridan had been very tight-lipped to learn that Spiffing Castle tours now featured ghosts and she was determined that the learning experience would not be vandalised by supernatural show-offs. After Lord Spiffing's welcoming speech, during which he had introduced Madam Moonbeam as his new tour assistant, Miss Harridan took him to one side and emphasised that education, not entertainment, was the focus of the visit. Would he please do everything in his power to ensure that the children did not see a ghost?

But Lord Spiffing fully intended the children to see a ghost; since Madam Moonbeam's arrival at the castle, Gerald had been popping up with reliable timeliness in the Great Hall to scare the pants off everybody – a non-appearance now would be bad for business. Besides, Miss Harridan looked exactly the sort of grumpy old bag who had made his own schooldays such a misery. He took the children's side on this one, so he said stiffly, 'I'm sorry, Miss Harridan, but I'm afraid I have absolutely no control over my Dear Departed.

Now then, before we begin, does anyone have a question?'

Tara put her hand up. 'Have you got bats?' she asked.

Lord Spiffing looked surprised. 'Have I gone bats?'

'I'd like a bat as a pet,' explained Tara.

Lord Spiffing looked relieved. 'Ah-ha,' he nodded. 'Yes, we've got heaps of bats. Please take as many as you like. Vile things, bats. Now, shall we hit the path, as they say? Come along, everyone.'

While the children were herded out of the entrance hall to begin the tour, Oli and Skipjack hung back, pretending to admire a very gloomy ancestral portrait.

'If I was related to someone as ugly as that,' whispered Skipjack, 'I certainly wouldn't put him on a wall for everyone to see.'

As soon as the hall was empty Skipjack reached into his backpack and produced the Spookoscope. He raised it over his thatch of hair. He paused. He held it out to Oli.

'You can go first, if you like,' he said, carelessly.

'OK, Skip,' said his friend. 'If you're sure.'

Oli pulled the Spookoscope firmly on to his head and was just wrestling with the chinstrap when a squeal of laughter burst across the hall. From behind two suits of armour appeared Tara and her friend Daisy Levity, giggling helplessly. Daisy was a pretty girl with shiny hair and big eyes who found much in life to giggle about.

'We guessed you'd try it as soon as you could, so we hid!' cried Daisy. 'You look like a mad scientist!'

'You are never going to see a ghost through that thing,' declared Tara, 'because Ghosts Don't Exist.'

This challenge provoked exactly the reaction she wanted.

'Wanna bet?' demanded her brother.

'Yes,' said Tara quickly. 'If you don't find a ghost you have to pay £10 into my Running Away to Africa Fund.'

As Oli's savings amounted to exactly this sum, he strongly suspected his sister of piggy-bank snooping. And as those precious coins had been scraped together to replace the favourite rugby ball he had kicked on to the roof, it was a high price to pay. But he couldn't back out now.

'OK, but if I do find a ghost,' he told her, 'you have to give me Triffid.'

Tara scowled. Triffid was the Venus Fly Trap she had nurtured from sprout-hood. She loved to catch bugs and drop them on to Triffid's trigger hairs. She loved to watch the bugs scuttle in vain between the slowly closing prison bars of Triffid's spiky lobes. She loved to imagine Triffid's poison dissolving them into soup. Most of all she loved to gloat over Oli's shrivelled attempts to grow his own Venus Fly Trap. But she couldn't back out now.

'All right, but Daisy and I have to see the ghost, too. Otherwise it doesn't count.' Then she cheered up. 'You won't win, anyhow.'

'Just you wait.' Oli put the goggles over his eyes.

'Make sure the Psychic Surge button's off,' Skipjack said anxiously. 'Remember Matt's warning.'

Oli checked that the red button on the control box was turned to zero and then, with a prickle of excitement, he switched on the Spookoscope.

'Well?' demanded Tara. 'Can you see anything?'

Oli peered through the goggles. 'Nothing at all,' he said, disappointed. 'Just the caretaker.'

'We can all see him,' said Tara, glancing at an old man sweeping near the front door. 'So he's obviously not a ghost.'

Oli looked at the control box in his hand. 'The dial's reading 50,' he said. 'There must be something about.'

'It's probably picking up electrical impulses from your brain,' said Tara.

Skipjack said cheerfully, 'I don't think my brain has any electrical impulses. Just pepperoni-pizza impulses.'

'Perhaps we need to go to a spookier bit of the castle?' suggested Oli. 'Look – the sign on that door says DUNGEON. There must be ghosts in a dungeon.'

'Face it, guys.' Tara shrugged. 'Ghosts Don't Exist.'

'In that case,' said Skipjack, 'I dare *you* to go down there with the Spookoscope.'

'I would, easily,' said Tara. 'Except I don't want to miss the tour. I bet *you* wouldn't dare, though.'

It was another challenge. Normally, Skipjack held the view that picking up challenges could lead to trouble of the scary sort, so he opened his mouth to tell Tara that she was quite right; he wouldn't go into the dungeon for a zillion pounds. But then he caught sight of Daisy. She was giggling at him.

History is littered with crazy things that have

been done to impress girls: Fire-breathing dragons have been slain, oceans overflowing with sea-monsters have been crossed and hostile tribes with a taste for roasted explorer have been tamed, just for a 'Wow' from a pretty face.

'Of course I'd dare,' said Skipjack.

'Wow,' squeaked Daisy.

'Good,' said Tara. 'To prove it you have to tell us how many steps there are to the bottom, and stay down there for a whole minute to give the Spookoscope a chance to work.'

'You'll be fine,' Oli told his friend, as he handed over the Spookoscope.

Skipjack pulled it on. 'I'll be fine,' he nodded, his antennae bouncing. 'It's just a cellar.'

'The Spookoscope doesn't work anyway,' Oli pointed out.

'It's totally useless. See you later.'

'Bye-bye, Skipjack,' called Daisy. 'Hope the ghosts don't get you!'

The girls ran away, dragging Oli with them and leaving the hall silent but for the fading echoes of their footsteps.

Skipjack pushed open the heavy, creaking

dungeon door. A set of stone steps spiralled down into darkness. The last thing Skipjack saw before he began his descent was the old caretaker, who had stopped sweeping and was watching him, shaking his head silently.

Down the dark and clammy steps crept Skipjack, with pounding heart and icy dread. His imagination painted looming monster-shadows on the walls and blew the chilly breath of hidden zombies down his neck. He shivered and concentrated on counting. At the foot of the stairs he groaned. Thirteen steps – just his luck.

I'll stay here for thirty seconds, thought Skipjack, and then I'll leg it. He followed the luminous hands of his watch, trying to focus on the ticking seconds and not on the growing sense that he was not alone. Something was there. A horrible smell was surging up around him like a tidal wave of dog-breath. He felt a sudden pressure in his left ear, as if he was deep under water. He looked down at the control box in his hand and was amazed to see that the dial had shot from zero to 60. Then he saw something else that gave him the biggest shock of all: the Psychic Surge button was turned to 'low'. His brother's words echoed in his head: 'It could do anything.' He tore off the Spookoscope and fled up the stairs.

Skipjack fell into the entrance hall and collided with Oli.

'I was just coming to get you,' said Oli.

'There's something down there!' panted Skipjack, thrusting the Spookoscope at him. 'The Psychic Surge button was turned on!'

'Great! But you've got to come quickly. The ghost is about to appear in the Great Hall.'

Skipjack shook his head. 'But I don't want to see a ghost! I've been spooked enough for a lifetime!'

'Well, I do and I haven't. You stay here, then.' Oli ran off with the Spookosope. Skipjack glanced behind him at the dungeon doorway, still wide open like the hungry mouth of the underworld. Realising in a flash that seeing a ghost with Oli and all the other children would be far less scary than *not* seeing a ghost all by himself, Skipjack ran to catch up with his friend. On the way to the Great Hall he explained what had happened in the dungeon.

'So basically it was a clammy feeling and a bad smell?' said Oli. 'I hate to say this, Skip, but that's pretty much what you always get in a cellar.'

'This wasn't a normal cellar smell. It was horrible – a kind of wild animal smell.'

'Like Slugger Stubbins after a rugby match?'

'Even worse. And the speedo shot right round to 60 thingies so it *must* have been a ghost!'

'OK,' said Oli. 'We'll go back later with the girls.'

They slipped in next to Tara and Daisy at the back of the crowd of children and Oli put the Spookoscope on again, turned the Psychic Surge button back to zero and flicked the 'on' switch.

Lord Spiffing was talking about the portrait of his great-great-grandfather, Gerald.

'And now for something very exciting, children: any minute now, Gerald himself will show up – on that balcony. A real, live ghost!

Well, not exactly live of course. Look – there he is!'

Sure enough, a pale, translucent figure appeared on the gallery. There was a scream of excitement from the children. Madam Moonbeam, standing at the back of the room with her remote control, decided to let the ghost float around for a bit longer this time as the children were so thrilled and Miss Harridan looked so delightfully cross. So Gerald lingered on the balcony for nearly a minute until a rubber ball was pinged at him from the crowd and whizzed straight through his head.

'Slugger Stubbins!' roared Miss Harridan. 'Hand over that catapult!'

As the ghost faded away, Oli took off the

Spookscope. He was frowning. 'That was weird,' he said. 'It didn't register at all. Perhaps I was standing too far away.'

'I don't think it was a real ghost,' announced Tara. 'Real ghosts never turn up exactly when they are told to.'

'I thought you didn't believe in real ghosts?' said her brother.

'Hello, hello?' warbled the voice of Lord Spiffing, trying to make himself heard over the babble.

'SILENCE,' boomed Miss Harridan on his behalf.

'Ah-ha. Thank you.' Lord Spiffing coughed. 'If everyone would be kind enough to follow me, we'll go on to the library.'

As they all trooped out of the Great Hall, Oli did a mental recap of the Spookoscope's tally so far:

- In the Entrance Hall: 1 spinning dial but no ghost seen through goggles.

- In the Dungeon (reported by Skipjack): 1

'strange smell and blocked ear' plus spinning dial, but no ghost seen.

- ❊ In the Great Hall: 1 ghost seen through goggles, but no spinning dial (and in any case ghost seen by everyone else *without* a Spookoscope).

All in all it was a disappointing result and Oli was beginning to wonder whether Spiffing Castle was ghostless after all, or the Spookoscope was a dud, or they simply did not have the necessary psychic skill. He decided to have one last go in the library. Standing at the back once again, so as to be behind Miss Harridan, he pulled the Spookoscope on, lowered the goggles and squinted through.

'GHOST!' he shouted.

Everyone screamed. Miss Harridan spun round, glaring. 'Oli!' she scolded. 'Is it you under that thing? How dare you interrupt Lord Spiffing with such a ridiculous fib!'

'It isn't a fib,' Oli insisted. He pointed towards the opposite end of the room. 'There really is a ghost – sitting over there with its feet up on the desk.'

Lord Spiffing turned to Madam Moonbeam. 'Is it true?' he whispered excitedly.

As Madam Moonbeam could not see this ghost or any other ghost, she followed the best line of defence, and attacked.

'No, Lord Spiffing, it is not true. The teacher is quite right; that boy is playing a practical joke on us all.'

Oli saw the ghost swoop over to Madam Moonbeam, waggle a finger in front of her nose and vanish.

'He's gone,' he said, disappointed. 'But I

promise it was a ghost. He started off in that chair and then he flew over to your assistant and shook his finger at her.'

A burst of laughter greeted this statement and the frowning Miss Harridan clapped her hands for silence. 'Go outside at once and eat your packed lunches.' She turned to the Spiffings. 'I do apologise. The boy will be punished, of course . . .'

'Nonsense, my dear lady,' beamed Lord Spiffing. 'This is splendid news. We're all in favour of ghosts here, aren't we, Agatha?'

'The more the merrier,' agreed his wife. 'Could we speak to the boy with the thing on his

head?'

So Oli, with Skipjack following in his wake, pushed through the outgoing tide of children to the spot where the Spiffings stood. Madam Moonbeam, meanwhile, slipped away through a side door before she could be asked any more awkward questions.

'How d'you do,' said Lord Spiffing, taking Oli's hand and giving it a good shake. 'I'm afraid I didn't catch your name?'

'Oli Biggles,' said Oli. 'And this is my friend Skipjack Haynes. His brother invented this ghost detector. We call it a Spookoscope.'

'He must be a genius. Tell us about the ghost you just saw.'

'Well, he had a big moustache,' said Oli, frowning to remember, 'and he was wearing uniform.'

'Well, I'm jiggered!' cried Lord Spiffing. 'You've just seen my Great-Uncle Bartholomew! No wonder he was teasing poor Madam Moonbeam – where's she gone? Agatha, dear, this boy's just seen Uncle Beetle! Do you know what this might mean?'

The normally calm Lady Spiffing was looking quite flushed. 'I do, Algy,' she cried. 'And I'm most excited!'

'So am I, Binky, so am I!'

Skipjack, who had been looking from one excited Spiffing to the other like a spectator at a tennis match, put up his hand.

'Excuse me, sir,' he said, 'But can you tell me and Oli why you're excited, so we can be excited, too?'

'I can tell you in one word, my boy: treasure!'

Skipjack nodded. 'We're excited.'

'That's awesome,' agreed Oli. 'What kind of treasure?'

Lord Spiffing cleared his throat and began. 'One hundred and fifty years ago last January, Bartholomew Philibert Spiffing was born. That's his portrait behind me.' He pointed to a full-length painting of a man draped in exotic robes and boasting moustaches which looked like a couple of hedgehogs glued to his upper lip. 'He was,' continued Lord Spiffing, 'my father's father's father's youngest brother's second son –'

'Algy dear,' interrupted his wife, 'You don't

need to start all the way back with Noah and the Ark.' She turned to the boys. 'Great-Uncle Bartholomew was an ancestor who spent lots of time in Egypt fighting the natives with General Gordon, and also collecting things. He was particularly fond of beetles – hence his nickname. This castle is full of beetles, most of them in display-cases, neatly pinned and labelled. But – and here's where it gets interesting – he also brought back something frightfully valuable.'

'What?' asked the boys.

'That's the problem. There was a family argument, so whatever it was, he hid it somewhere. He died soon afterwards – most unhelpful of him. He crashed his flying machine into the north wall. Since then no one has ever known what to look for, or where to look for it. The treasure could be a necklace or a pot or anything in between; it could be buried under the rose bed or hidden behind a secret panel.'

'Didn't he leave any clues?' asked Oli. 'Like a map, or something?'

Lord Spiffing gave a wry smile. 'Oh, yes, he left clues. We've found riddles and plans galore over the years, but they've all been red herrings.'

'Red herrings?' asked Skipjack, wondering how fish had swum into the story.

'False trails,' explained Lady Spiffing. 'Remember the time we found the map of the lake, Algy, with X marking the spot right in the middle? We bought diving tanks and flippers and spent a whole summer upside-down, poking about in the mud like a pair of ducks. Never found a thing.'

'We found my old bicycle,' corrected Lord Spiffing. 'And anyway, it was rather fun.'

'They've all been rather fun,' agreed his wife, 'but none of them have led to the treasure.'

'That's why we're so excited about your marvellous hat,' explained Lord Spiffing. 'If we could use it to talk to Uncle Beetle, we could persuade him to tell us where the treasure is. Then at least we could have the roof repaired and we wouldn't have to sleep in raincoats any more.'

'So would you mind lending it to us, just for a few days?' asked Lady Spiffing.

Skipjack shook his head with vigour. 'I'm sorry, but my brother comes home on Sunday evening and if he finds out I've borrowed his Spookoscope I'll be dead. If he finds out I've lent it to you, I'll be dead in a really slow, squelchy way.'

'Well, why don't the two of you come and stay for the weekend?' suggested Lady Spiffing. 'Then you can use the magic hat yourselves. You'd be much better at ghost-detecting than us old folks anyway. And we'll make sure you get home before your brother.'

To Oli this sounded a wonderful idea, but Skipjack looked appalled, as if Count Dracula had just said, 'Come and share my coffin.'

Lady Spiffing said quickly, 'Why don't you talk it over between you, and of course you'll have to ask your parents. You can let us know later.'

'Thank you,' said Oli. 'We'd better go and have our lunch now.'

As soon as they were out of range he turned to his friend. 'What's up, Skip? A real treasure hunt and a chance to win my bet with Tara – this could be awesome!'

'There's no way I'm spending a night here,' announced Skipjack as he marched through the hall towards the garden door. 'Not with that ghost in the dungeon.'

'You can't turn down the chance of a lifetime just because of a bad smell,' objected Oli.

'It's not the chance of a lifetime – it's the chance of a death-time!' cried Skipjack.

Oli sighed. 'All right, I promise we won't go near the dungeon. Now will you say yes?'

'You don't believe in my ghost, I can tell,' said Skipjack. 'You think I'm just imagining it.'

Oli frowned at the floor. It was true that he didn't take Skipjack's ghost very seriously. Skipjack had the kind of imagination that ran away with an idea like a dog ran away with a bone.

Then a voice murmured close to Oli's ear: 'He's telling the truth, you know. There was a ghost in the dungeon. It was me.'

Oli spun round, but there was no one there. Apart from Skipjack, of course, who was looking spookily pale himself.

'You . . . you heard it too, didn't you?' he stammered. 'That voice?'

Oli nodded. 'Who was it?'

'Who was it?' echoed the voice, above them now. 'Oh, it's only *Norman*. "Norman doesn't matter. Norman just smells." '

'You do smell!' shouted Skipjack, holding his nose and looking all around for a body to go with the voice. 'Go away, Norman, whoever you are! Leave us alone!'

'That's just what *they* said,' whispered Norman, behind them now. ' "Go away, Norman – you'll spoil our game. Mummy, make Norman go away. We don't want him to play with us." '

'This is too weird,' muttered Oli and ripped off the Spookoscope. 'I've had enough. Let's go.' He grabbed Skipjack's arm and pulled him towards the garden door. Skipjack stumbled after him, casting fearful glances over his shoulder.

Outside, they sprinted through the big, grassy garden dotted with picnicking children until they reached a tree in the far corner. Here, a safe distance from the castle and Norman, they flopped down on the sun-dappled grass. It was several moments before either of them had enough breath to speak.

'In a lifetime of scary things happening to me,

that was way the scariest,' declared Skipjack. 'Scarier than being shouted at by Mr Grimble, scarier than science tests, scarier than running out of triple-pepperoni pizza.'

'I suppose after Norman you definitely don't want to come back this weekend to hunt for the treasure,' said Oli.

'Definitely is the word,' agreed Skipjack.

'It's weird that you could hear him without the Spookoscope,' remarked Oli. 'But maybe Norman is just a ghost that everyone can hear, like Gerald in the Great Hall is a ghost that everyone can see.'

'Do you think the Spiffings know he's haunting the castle?' asked Skipjack.

But then he heard the voice again, in an evil whisper:

'I'm not haunting the castle, Skipjack. I'm haunting YOU!'

Skipjack leapt up. 'Stop it!' he shouted.

'Stop what, Skip?'

'It's him again! He's come after us!'

'But I can't hear anything,' Oli objected.

'You must be able to – he's right here!'

'Come on, we'll run away again,' said Oli.

Yes, run, Skipjack,' taunted Norman in his ear. 'Let's play tag. I'll be it. I'll count to ten. One, two . . .'

Skipjack blocked his ears. 'Bibble-bibble-bibble!' he shouted, but it was not enough to keep out Norman's voice:

'But wherever you run, Skipjack. I'll just come with you. You can never escape.'

Skipjack lowered his hands. 'It's no good, Oli,' he said miserably. 'I'm stuck with him. I wish you'd put on the Spookoscope so I don't have to hear him all by myself.'

The last thing in the universe that Oli wanted to do was hear – and smell – Norman, but he couldn't leave his friend alone with such a horrible visitation. So he pulled on the Spookoscope, making sure the Psychic Surge button was firmly off.

Norman was speaking, in his high, whining voice. '*They* never let me play tag when we were little. They said I was nasty. Then later they said I was mad. Then I died and they thought they were well rid of me.'

'I can see how they would think that,' remarked Oli, holding his nose.

'Oh, can you?' said Norman sharply. 'Well, I'm back now, thanks to your friend.'

'Why thanks to me?' asked Skipjack.

'Because you pulled me out of the ecto-dimension.'

'What on earth is the ecto-dimension?' asked Oli.

'It's not *on* earth at all, Thicko,' said Norman. 'It's where ghosts live – where I've been for the last forty years. I was so desperate to get back here and punish everyone – to haunt them, to terrify them in the night. But I could never get through the divide. Then all of a sudden, you came along, Skipjack, with that machine of yours and you must have opened up a psychic pathway. I could feel myself being drawn, as if by a magnet. I realised you were pulling me out of the ecto-dimension. So I let go, and slipped through the divide. If only you had kept the machine on for a few more moments I would have been able to get,' he whispered close to Skipjack's ear, 'right inside your head.'

Skipjack shuddered.

'As it is,' sighed Norman, 'I'll just have to

haunt you for ever and ever. Believe me, I wish it could be someone else. Even from here I can see that your brain contains almost nothing but rugby and pizza.'

Skipjack wanted to demand what was wrong with rugby and pizza but he was too scared.

'Luckily for you,' Norman went on, 'I don't want to haunt you for ever and ever. I only want to haunt you until you can get me where I really want to be.'

Skipjack glimpsed a speck of hope. 'Where's that?' he asked.

'Inside Lord Spiffing's head.'

'What for?'

'Revenge,' said Norman simply. 'For forty very long years I've watched my cousin Algernon lead his easy, happy, charming life. He was one of them, you know. One of the ones who wouldn't let me play, who laughed at me and called me names. Now I want my own back. I want you to get me inside Algernon Spiffing's head. I want to make his life hell on earth. I want to give him nightmares that will have him screaming – Eeek!'

'DON'T do that!' cried Skipjack, clapping his

hands over his ears.

'So, Skipjack, there's your escape. Get me into my cousin's head. If you succeed, you will be rid of me. If you fail, I will haunt you for ever. You have until nightfall on Saturday. Goodbye.'

It was some time before either of the boys spoke.

'D'you think he's gone?' whispered Skipjack.

'I think so,' replied Oli in a low voice. 'For now, anyway. Phew.' He pulled off the Spookoscope.

'Oh, Oli,' moaned Skipjack. 'This is like a horror movie – it's worse than a horror movie, cos in horror movies it's not happening to *me*. If only I had checked that blogging red button before I put the Spookoscope on.'

'Now we've really got to come back this weekend,' said Oli. 'If we can find out more about Norman we might find a way to get rid of him, and in the worst case we can pass him on to Lord Spiffing.'

'How?' asked Skipjack.

'We'll have to get Lord Spiffing to try on the Spookoscope with the Psychic Surge button turned up. Poor Lord Spiffing.'

'Huh! If poor Lord Spiffing had been nicer to Norman when they were little, I wouldn't be starring in "Revenge of the Stink-Ghost" right now.'

The boys debated whether to tell Tara and Daisy about Norman but decided against this for three reasons:

1 The girls would not believe them;

2 If their parents heard of anything scary at the castle they might not allow the weekend visit; and

3 If Lord Spiffing learnt about Norman's intentions he would never put on the Spookoscope and their plans would be trashed.

So instead they spent the homeward journey discussing the Spiffings' invitation to return at the weekend for a treasure hunt. The girls were, of course, deeply sceptical about Uncle Beetle.

‘What will it take to convince you two?’ demanded Oli.

‘We’ve already told you,’ shrugged Tara. ‘We have to see a ghost with our own eyes. Then you win the bet.’

‘Would smelling a ghost be enough?’ Oli asked.

‘No.’

‘*Hearing* a ghost?’

‘Maybe.’

‘Being carried off by a ghost to the ecto-dimension?’

‘Don’t be silly.’

'So how was the trip to the castle?' asked Mrs Biggles over supper that evening.

'Great,' said Oli.

'They've got bats,' said Tara, 'but I didn't see any.'

'What were Lord and Lady Spiffing like?'

'Really nice,' said Oli. 'In fact, they've asked Skipjack and me to go back this weekend and help them find some treasure. Can we go?' He crossed his fingers under the table.

'How exciting,' said Mum. 'Why you and Skipjack?'

Oli shrugged carelessly. 'I dunno. We got chatting to them and I guess they must have liked us. They said we'd be much better at treasure-hunting than them, cos they're so old.'

Tara opened her mouth to say something, and

then closed it again. Where there were secrets, there was Silence Money to be made. Her Running Away to Africa Fund had not recovered since the unfortunate incident of the stray cat, the frogspawn and Mum's laptop. She popped a meatball in her mouth and chewed thoughtfully.

Oli was pressing on. 'Well, Mum?'

Like most of the town, Mrs Biggles regarded the Spiffings as nuttier than a pair of pecan pies, but otherwise harmless. So she said, 'Of course you can go.'

'Will you catch me a bat?' asked Tara.

Mum shuddered. 'If there's one thing this house doesn't need, it's a bat.'

'Unless it's a cricket bat,' put in Oli, who had been angling for a new one.

'Cricket's boring,' declared Tara.

'No, you're boring,' retorted Oli.

'Enough,' said Mum. 'Up to bed.'

In the bathroom, Tara cornered her brother with her accusations sharpened.

'You didn't tell Mum the truth about seeing Uncle Beetle's ghost through the Spookoscope,' she said.

'But according to you and Daisy,' he replied, 'I didn't see him, cos ghosts don't exist . . . Nightie-night.' And he sauntered away to his bedroom, whistling and fighting down the urge to punch the air.

* * *

The sun was setting behind Spiffing Castle as the boys approached on Friday evening, in the back of Skipjack's dad's car. Long black shadows stretched across the park as if reaching out, thought Skipjack, to pounce at intruders. They parked in the yard and climbed out into a hairy welcoming party of tall, thin dogs. Lord and Lady Spiffing, also tall and thin but less hairy, pushed through the wagging thicket to welcome their visitors.

'We're jolly pleased you're here,' beamed Lord Spiffing as they waved goodbye to Skipjack's dad. 'We haven't seen Uncle Beetle again; not even Madam Moonbeam has.'

'Your tour assistant?'

'Ah. We need to tell you about that. The lady you saw during your visit yesterday is not in fact a tour assistant; she's a clairvoyant.'

Both boys looked blank. 'A Claire who?' asked Oli.

'A clairvoyant is someone who can talk to ghosts,' explained Lady Spiffing. 'We invited her here to rally up Algy's Dear Departed for the tourists. It was Madam Moonbeam who encouraged Great-Great-Grandfather Gerald to appear on the balcony.'

'So, Gerald is a real ghost?' asked Skipjack, thinking of Tara and Daisy's suspicions.

'Of course,' said Lord Spiffing. 'I can't tell you how excited we were when he first appeared.'

'But we're even more excited about Uncle Beetle,' added his wife. 'Let's take your bags in and go straight to the library to see if you can find him again with your magic hat.'

So a keen troop of ghost-hunters, led by Lord Spiffing and several dogs, set off through the castle. As they approached the door to the Great Hall, through which they had to pass to reach the library, both boys heard the patter of retreating feet and when they arrived at their destination a few seconds later, a strange sight was ready for them.

Madam Moonbeam was standing in the middle of the room with her eyes closed and her

arms stretched out to the side, looking like an over-stuffed purple scarecrow.

Lord Spiffing peered at her. 'Are you feeling quite all right, Madam Moonbeam?'

'This is my Psychic Trance Position,' she whispered. 'I am communicating with the spirits.' Now her eyes flickered open and looked beyond Lord Spiffing to where the boys stood with the Spookoscope. Gasping as if struck by a sudden pain, she clutched her heart and collapsed into the nearest chair.

A look of concern crumpled Lord Spiffing's face. 'Madam Moonbeam – are you quite all right?'

'I sense unease among the spirits,' she murmured, 'At the return of the Contraption.'

'Which one of us is the contraption?' muttered Skipjack to Oli. 'You or me?'

'I think she means the Spookoscope,' Oli muttered back.

'Well, we need the contraption to find the treasure,' said Lady Spiffing briskly. 'So the spirits will just have to lump it. Are you ready to do your stuff, Oli?'

Oli checked the Psychic Surge button and pulled on the Spookoscope. He adjusted the goggles, peered round the room and gave a snort of laughter.

'Can you see Uncle Beetle?' asked Lord Spiffing eagerly.

'Yes, I can,' said Oli. 'He's hanging upside-down in front of Madam Moonbeam, pulling faces.'

'I wish I could see,' giggled Skipjack. The Spiffings were chuckling too. Even the dogs seemed to be laughing. The whole library positively glowed with warmth and jollity.

Only Madam Moonbeam failed to see the funny side. She was annoyed at being teased by an invisible ghost and laughed at by two little kids. She was also annoyed that her position as Number One Ghost Producer was under direct threat from Oli and his ridiculous contraption. So she said, 'I hope this boy is not deceiving you, Lord Spiffing. It is very strange that I, with all my *genuine* powers, should not feel any spiritual presence.'

'Genuine powers – ha!' scoffed Uncle Beetle as he turned the right way up. 'The only thing of yours that is genuine, madam, is your talent for pretending.'

'I can hear you, too!' cried Oli.

'Can you?' Uncle Beetle swooped in for a good look at the character in the funny hat. 'You must be very special. No one's been able to hear me for a hundred years. And I've had so much to say. What's your name?'

'Oli Biggles,' said Oli. 'And this is my friend, Skipjack. But he can't hear you, not without the Spookoscope and he's never trying that again.'

'I should think not,' agreed Uncle Beetle. 'I

heard about that. Nasty business.'

'Ask him about the treasure,' hissed Lord Spiffing.

'Can you hear him as well?' Oli asked Uncle Beetle. 'Or can you just hear me cos I'm wearing the Spookoscope?'

'Is that the Spookoscope? I thought it was a fashionable hat. Yes, I can hear him. I can hear all of them, although there are some people I would much rather *not* hear.' And he flew over to glare into Madam Moonbeam's face. Oli giggled again.

'What's he doing now?' demanded Madam Moonbeam, flapping her arms about as if swatting away a fly.

'If you can hear them,' said Oli to the ghost, 'then you'll know that they really want to find your treasure, so they can sell it and mend the roof.'

Uncle Beetle chuckled. 'I do know. They've been hunting for long enough.'

'Will you tell me where it is?'

'I might not want them to sell my treasure,' Uncle Beetle pointed out. 'I might like my treasure. On the other hand, I might not even *have* any treasure. And I might be feeling just a little bit hurt that *some* people don't even believe I exist. So I might need to think about it. Anyway, I haven't had so much attention for a century so I'm jolly well going to make the most of it. Pip-pip.'

And he disappeared.

'He's gone,' said Oli and took off the Spookoscope.

'What a fantastic hat that is,' marvelled Lord Spiffing. 'May I have a look at it?'

Oli flashed a glance at Skipjack and held out the Spookoscope. Could this be the moment Norman had been waiting for?

Lord Spiffing turned it over in his hands. 'Well, I'm jiggered – it's a scrum cap, isn't it? I used to play in the second row myself, but scrum caps didn't look like this in my day. May I try it on?'

'Er, it's Skipjack's . . .' Oli said uncertainly.

Lord Spiffing turned to Skipjack. 'May I?'

Learning that the person on whom he was trying to inflict the poisonous Norman had been a rugby player threw Skipjack into a whirlpool of guilt and indecision. He bent to pat the nearest dog while he did a super-quick eeny-meeny-miney-mo in his head. But the dog suddenly whined and scampered away to the door, where he was joined by all his pals in a sudden chorus of howling.

'Mice again,' explained Lady Spiffing over the din and she opened the door to let the dogs clatter out into the passage.

But Skipjack's nose told him the real reason for the canine exodus, and seconds later a familiar voice hissed in his left ear, 'Remember, Skipjack: For ever is a very long time.'

So he looked up at Lord Spiffing and said unhappily, 'Yes.' Then he held his breath as his victim pulled on the Spookoscope.

'STOP!' cried Madam Moonbeam.

Lord Spiffing, who always obeyed commands from the women in his life, stopped.

Madam Moonbeam decided that some Acting was now called for. Recalling her famous performance in *The Death of Cleopatra*, she staggered over to Lord Spiffing, gripping the furniture and moaning.

'Please, Lord Spiffing,' she gasped. 'Don't make your Dear Departed even angrier. For you, of all people, to put on this, this . . . *thing* would risk making enemies of every one of them, including Great-Uncle Bartholomew.'

As Great-Uncle Bartholomew alone stood between the Spiffings and Desperate Measures this was a powerful argument. Lord Spiffing removed the Spookoscope with a sigh and handed it back to Oli, while Skipjack glared at Madam Moonbeam and wished he had a machine gun.

'Well, did old Uncle B say anything about the treasure?' asked His Lordship.

'Er, no. Not this time,' said Oli.

'And he never will, believe me,' put in Madam Moonbeam. 'They have pride, your ancestors. This wicked contraption –'

'Dear Madam Moonbeam,' said Lady Spiffing. 'I wonder if you could possibly have another try with the ghost of the Blue Lady in the drawing room? I feel sure that with your skill and sensitivity you must be so close to making contact with her.'

Violet Moonbeam smiled modestly. 'I am indeed very close, Your Ladyship,' she purred, and she floated away. No sooner was she outside the door, however, than her tranquil smile was replaced by a dark scowl. Drat those boys and drat their contraption. Very soon Lord Spiffing was bound to see Uncle Beetle too, or they would find out where the treasure was hidden, or both. Either way she would be packing her bags and returning to her tiny flat. Something would have to be done.

'You mustn't mind Madam Moonbeam,' said Lady Spiffing to the boys. 'She's just anxious that we might think less of her now that you are here with your magic hat. I think we should leave Uncle Beetle in peace – we can have another go in the morning. Have you boys had supper yet?'

'Yes,' said Oli.

'No,' said Skipjack at the same time and nudged his friend.

'I mean, no,' said Oli, hoping it would be worth it.

'You're in for a treat, then,' beamed Lady Spiffing. 'Algernon has cooked his special corned beef and potato hash.'

Now it was Oli's turn to nudge Skipjack, hard. On his scale of treats, corned beef had always ranked somewhere below boiled cabbage. But there was no escape now.

Lord Spiffing led the way to the kitchen where he produced, from deep inside the ancient cooking range, a big black frying pan.

'Help yourselves to ketchup and tuck in,' urged

the cook proudly as he piled everyone's plate high with sizzling hash.

Oli took a small forkful and chewed tentatively. To his surprise, it was delicious. 'I never knew corned beef could taste like this,' he marvelled.

'It's really yummy,' agreed Skipjack, squirting his initials on to his plate in ketchup.

Lord Spiffing beamed. 'The secret is to get it good and crispy. Madam Moonbeam won't touch it – she says it's so unhealthy she's surprised we haven't already joined our Dear Departed. I told her about the ketchup, but she says ketchup doesn't count either. She forgets it's full of tomatoes.'

The boys felt a deep bond with Lord Spiffing. Here was a man with whom they shared so much: a favourite sport (rugby) and a favourite vegetable (tomato ketchup), all of which made Skipjack feel even more guilty about sharing his least-favourite ghost (Norman).

'If Madam Moonbeam isn't eating with us, who's the fifth place for?' asked Oli.

'Mrs Edwards, the housekeeper,' said Lady Spiffing.

'Is she coming later?'

'No, she's there now. She doesn't eat anything, but she likes to be included. She makes a terrible mess in here at night if we forget to lay a place for her.'

Skipjack's eyes widened. 'Mrs Edwards is a *ghost*?'

'That's right, dear.'

Skipjack gulped and shovelled down the rest of his hash with his eyes glued to the empty chair.

'Will you tell us more about Great-Uncle Bartholomew?' asked Oli.

'Oh, Uncle Beetle was a hoot,' chuckled Lord Spiffing. 'Still is, even dead. Last year he amused himself no end by locking all our lavatory doors from the inside, so no one could get in when they, er, needed to.'

'We had to fetch ladders and climb in through the windows,' added Lady Spiffing. 'In the end we hid away all the keys, so now you have to sing loudly.'

'He doesn't seem to like Madam Moonbeam much,' remarked Oli.

'I suspect he knows that she would disapprove of him,' said Lady Spiffing. 'He was quite an adventurer, and a famous card-player, too. Snap was his favourite. He won – and lost – a fortune. Now, has everyone finished? Who would like a mug of hot chocolate?'

Tara was spending Friday night with Daisy at her grandfather's cottage. The two girls had passed a happy evening lying on the floor of Daisy's room leafing through piles of joke-shop catalogues and planning all the things they would buy if they were millionaires.

'Except if we were millionaires we wouldn't want any of this,' Daisy pointed out. 'I know that, cos Grandad is always wishing that more millionaires would visit his shop.'

'In that case I never want to be a millionaire,' said Tara. She turned over another page and glanced at the picture. It showed a tiny remote-control camera, from which a ghostly image was being projected on to a wall. Tara frowned.

'Look at this.'

Daisy looked closely at the photo.

'That's the ghost in the Great Hall,' she said.

'Gerald,' agreed Tara. 'Except this shows it isn't Gerald at all; it's just an image from a camera.'

'Which means Gerald isn't a real ghost and we were right all along,' said Daisy, pleased.

'It also means the Spiffings are up to something,' frowned Tara. 'We must warn the boys.'

When Oli and Skipjack had slurped the last dregs of chocolate from the bottom of their mugs, Lady Spiffing suggested it might be time for bed.

'I'll find you some candles,' she said, rising from the table.

The boys exchanged glances. 'Er, why candles?' asked Oli.

'We never got around to installing electricity upstairs,' explained Lord Spiffing. 'Frightfully expensive in a place this size and quite unnecessary when one spends most of the time up there asleep.'

Skipjack was sure he wasn't going to spend

any time up there asleep, especially with no comforting light-switch by his bed. He would spend the whole night wide awake, peering anxiously over his blanket into the darkness and listening out for Norman.

'Besides, no electricity is more fun,' declared Lady Spiffing, striking a match and lighting two candles in red enamel holders. She placed a glass cover over each one to protect the flame and picked up the holders by their little handles. 'Up we go,' she said.

Leaving Lord Spiffing to roll up his sleeves and tackle the dirty dishes, she led the boys out of the kitchen. But when they reached the hall where their bags had been left, Skipjack slammed on his brakes.

'The Spookoscope!' he cried. 'It's gone!'

'Gone?' echoed Oli.

'I left it here on my bag when we came out of the library, and it's not here!' Skipjack began to rummage violently through his belongings, scattering a hailstorm of socks and toffees all over the hall. Finally he sat back on his heels. 'Gone.'

'Ah, here you all are!' Madam Moonbeam's voice floated down from above as she descended the wide staircase, purple scarves trailing in the breeze. 'Lady Spiffing,' she panted eagerly, 'I bring news from The Other Side!'

'How interesting,' said Lady Spiffing. 'The other side of what?'

Madam Moonbeam looked taken-aback. '*The* Other Side,' she explained. 'I was reclining in my bedroom, allowing messages from all the Dear Departed to flow through me, when I received a very clear communication from none other than Great-Uncle Bartholomew.'

'Really?' Lady Spiffing couldn't help looking doubtful.

Madam Moonbeam nodded vigorously. 'Yes, indeed. He says that in order to protect the privacy of all the castle spirits, he has hidden the wicked contraption.'

'I'm doomed!' groaned Skipjack. 'Now I'll never get rid of Nor–'

'How dare he steal our Spookoscope!' interrupted Oli quickly.

Violet Moonbeam aimed a stony eye at him.

'On the contrary, young man – how dare *you* arouse the anger of the Dear Departed. Lady Spiffing, I dread to think how the spirits will torment us if these boys do not leave them in peace.' And she gave a universal shudder, like a giant blackberry blancmange in an earthquake.

Poor Skipjack was dreading to think how Norman would torment *him* if they didn't find the Spookoscope. 'We've got to look for it,' he said through gritted teeth.

'Great-Uncle Bartholomew tells me,' said Madam Moonbeam hastily, 'that he has hidden it in a secret place where it can't possibly be found.'

'Perhaps he's put it with the treasure?' said Lady Spiffing.

Violet Moonbeam hadn't thought of this and now it struck her as a very good idea. If the Spiffings didn't find the treasure they would need her to stay and rally up more ghosts, and if they didn't find the Spookoscope they would have to send the boys home. So she said in a solemn voice,

'That is exactly what he hinted at.'

'Well, this is a fine state of affairs,' sighed Lady Spiffing. 'We need the magic hat to find the treasure but we need to know where the treasure is to find the magic hat. Well, there's nothing to be done now. We'll start looking in the morning.'

The loss of the Spookoscope weighed poor Skipjack down so heavily with gloom that he could hardly drag himself up the stairs. Lady Spiffing turned to them both at the top and asked, 'What kind of room would you like – haunted or not haunted?'

Oli would have enjoyed a haunted room but he doubted that his friend's nerves could take much more ghostery, so he said, 'Not haunted, please.'

'You'd better have the Egyptian room, then,' said Lady Spiffing and led the way to a wood-panelled room containing two four-poster beds opposite one another and a large red carpet in the middle. 'No one's ever seen a ghost in here,' she said, placing a candle on each bedside table. 'The nearest bathroom is at the end of the corridor on the left. And don't worry about your magic hat, Skipjack. We're sure to find it before your brother comes home on Sunday. Good night, sleep tight.'

As soon as they were alone Skipjack collapsed on his bed. 'I'd forgotten about Matt,' he sighed. 'I'm double doomed.' He gave a sniff, and remarked, 'No wonder the ghosts don't come here; it stinks of drains.'

Oli had taken his candle on a lap of the room and was holding it up to examine maps of the Nile and papyrus paintings of dog-headed people in short skirts. He sniffed. 'I can't smell anything.'

'Oh, no,' groaned Skipjack. 'That means –'

'Norman's here!' shrilled a voice in the darkness.

'Go away!' yelled Skipjack, burying his head under his pillow.

'Is it Norman again?' asked Oli.

'I want to go away,' said Norman. 'But I must say you're not helping much.'

'That's not my fault!' protested Skipjack, coming up for air. 'I wasn't the one who told Lord Spiffing to take off the Spookoscope and I wasn't the one who stole it!'

'Ask him if he knows where it's been hidden,' said Oli.

'I've no idea where it is,' sniffed Norman. 'Nobody tells me anything. They all ignore me, just like when I was solid. Believe me, I'd tell you if I knew. I don't want to be stuck with you any more than you want to be stuck with me. So you'd better find it, fast.'

There was a moment's silence and then Oli asked, 'Has he gone?'

'I think so.' Skipjack sounded bleak. 'If we don't find that Spookoscope I'm done for, Oli. I'll be haunted for ever by Norman, and murdered by my own brother in a slow, squelchy way.'

'Look on the bright side,' said Oli. 'If Matt murders you, Norman won't be able to haunt you any more, cos you'll be a ghost too.'

'Thanks Oli. You really know how to cheer a guy up.'

'Sorry. Tell you what, let's sneak out later tonight and hunt for it. Why wait until morning?'

Now, urgent as Skipjack's need for the Spookoscope was, he had no wish to creep around a dark and spooky castle stuffed with ghosts in the middle of the night. He racked his brain for an excuse. 'Er, it'll be too dark to find the Spookoscope with just our candles,' he said.

'Ta-da!' said Oli, producing his torch.

This offered no comfort to Skipjack who knew that beyond the puny beam of Oli's torch there would still be a whole heap of castle, dark and spooky and stuffed with ghosts. Then another thought struck him and he said, 'Uncle Beetle might have taken it into the ecto-dimension.'

But Oli only laughed. 'You sound like Madam Moonbeam. Come on – how about a game of rugby to take your mind off everything? Look, we've even got posts. The end of the bed is the try-line.'

So the two boys played an energetic game of one-aside until they judged that the castle's other inmates would be safely in bed. Then, armed with Oli's torch, they crept out into the corridor.

'How are we going to get in?' asked Daisy as they stashed their bicycles behind a bush near the back door of the castle.

'The key will be under the flowerpot,' whispered Tara. 'It always is.'

Daisy tipped back a big pot of geraniums and felt about underneath. 'Got it,' she whispered. She fitted the key in the lock, turned it, and pushed the door open.

At once there was a volley of barks from somewhere nearby, accompanied by the thuds of furry bodies flinging themselves against a door.

'Shut up, dogs!' hissed Tara. 'You'll wake up the whole castle!'

'We'd better be on the lookout,' whispered Daisy. She relocked the back door behind them and pocketed the key. 'Let's find the stairs.'

* * *

'Did you hear that barking?' Skipjack asked Oli. 'We'd better be on the lookout. Where are we going, anyway?'

'Let's start in the nearest bathroom,' whispered Oli.

'Which way is that? They should make road maps of places like this.'

'I think it's this way,' said Oli, 'but I'm not sure. Everything looks different in the dark.'

After they had crept along for a while Oli whispered, 'I think we've come the wrong way. I don't remember that curtain across the corridor.'

'Let's see if we recognise what's on the other side,' said Skipjack. He found the gap between the thickly hanging curtains and pulled them apart.

'ARGH!' he screamed, for just on the other side, less than a metre away, was a ghastly white vision waving an enormous axe.

'ARGH!' screamed the vision. It was then that Skipjack realised he was standing eyeball to googly eyeball with Lord Spiffing.

'I . . . I didn't recognise you,' stammered the boy, taking in the nightshirt and the long stripy cap. 'I thought you were another ghost.'

'I do apologise,' said His Lordship. 'I didn't mean to startle you like that. I heard the dogs barking, so I came to investigate.'

He saw Skipjack's gaze turn to the weapon he was gripping and held it out for the boy to see.

'This is my trusty Viking battle-axe,' he explained proudly. 'Still got the blood of Celtic rebels on it, see? So what brought you two out and about tonight?'

'Oh, er, we heard the dogs as well,' said Oli. 'But seeing as you're properly armed and we're not, we'll leave the investigating to you. Good night.'

Skipjack added, '*Please* come and tell us if you chop someone's head off.'

The Viking who had originally split Celtic skulls with Lord Spiffing's battle-axe would have been scornful to see it now being used as a walking stick, but the stairs were dark and His Lordship wobbly. So when Tara and Daisy crossed the hall, they were alerted to his approach by a timid tapping sound and had plenty of time to hide behind the two suits of armour before he arrived on the bottom step.

Such was Lord Spiffing's faith in his weapon that he was disappointed when a keen search of the ground floor unearthed no intruders against whom to wield it. Feeling rather flat, he returned to bed via the creaky back stairs.

The girls crept out from behind their suits of armour and were just tiptoeing towards the stairs when a movement near the enormous front door caught Tara's attention. She turned her head and then froze. The old caretaker, whom they had seen on their first visit, had appeared once more with his broom. It was too late to hide, but the caretaker only paused to shake his head solemnly at them before sweeping his way into the gloom of the kitchen passage.

'Thank goodness he didn't give us away,' whispered Daisy.

‘Perhaps he knows there’s something going on here and he wants to give us a chance to find out what,’ suggested Tara.

She was about to put a foot on the bottom stair when the fall of a shadow across the moonlit hall made them look up. Creeping down the staircase was a large woman in a shiny purple dressing gown. The girls recognised her as the Spiffings’ tour assistant Madam Moonbeam and they scuttled back to their suits of armour.

‘Doesn’t *anybody* ever sleep in this place?’ Tara wondered.

At first the girls feared they had been

spotted, for Madam Moonbeam bore down on them like an ocean liner, but at the last minute she veered left into the Great Hall.

Madam Moonbeam was on a mission: to check that the Gerald-projector was still charged up and securely taped to the wall behind the door. She had filled her pockets with the necessary tools and taken the precaution of locking the boys' bedroom door on her way past. She had also brought down the Spookoscope, with the intention of giving it a secret test drive in the library afterwards.

Eager to see what was occurring in the Great Hall, Tara crept out of hiding and peeked through a crack in the door. Then, still unable to see Madam Moonbeam, she pushed the door slightly wider ajar and stepped over the threshold.

Behind the door, holding her scissors and tape, Madam Moonbeam didn't move a muscle. Her first thought was that the intruder was one of the boys, but then she remembered she had locked them in their room. Could it be a Spiffing? No, neither of them could stand so still without rattling or wheezing. A sudden thrill shot through Madam Moonbeam – perhaps it was a ghost! Just then, the moon sailed out from behind a cloud, throwing broad silvery stripes through the castle windows on to the black floors. In one of these bright panels, the silhouette of Tara appeared across the floor of the Great Hall. In another stretched the huge shadow of Madam Moonbeam, holding a terrifyingly magnified pair of scissors.

Tara gasped, but before she could move the door behind her shut with a click. A fat hand was placed over her mouth. The hand smelled of lavender and Tara tried to bite it.

Madam Moonbeam whipped off her dressing gown cord and lashed it around Tara's middle, pinning the girl's arms to her sides. Then she cut a piece of tape from her roll and slapped it over Tara's mouth.

'Just in case,' she muttered.

'Mmmmmmm!' said Tara, outraged.

'Sorry, dear. I'm going to lock you in the tower while I decide what to do with you. It'll teach you to spy on your elders and betters.'

So the furious Tara, trussed up like a chicken, was hoisted over Madam Moonbeam's shoulder and carried away. As she bumped along she wondered how Daisy would set about rescuing her and whether in the meantime there would be any bats in the tower that she could catch and smuggle home.

* * *

Oli and Skipjack had given Lord Spiffing plenty of time to chop up intruders and go back to bed before deciding to venture out of their room again. But they had come up against an obstacle straight away, in the very solid shape of a locked bedroom door.

'How did that happen?' wondered Skipjack.

'Someone doesn't want us snooping around,' replied Oli. 'Question is: who?'

'Answer is: the same traitor who took the Spookoscope,' said Skipjack. 'Your good friend Uncle Beetle.'

'I think that's rubbish,' said Oli. 'For one thing, he really likes the Spookoscope, cos he can chat to people, and for another thing he really *doesn't* like Madam Moonbeam, so she's the last person he'd tell if he did take it. Also, he says she isn't a real Claire-whatsit; she's just pretending. That explains why she can't see him.'

Skipjack's eyes widened. 'You think she pinched the Spookoscope herself – the old cow! Thanks to her, I might be lumbered with Nasty

Norman for ever.'

'At least we know it hasn't been taken into the ecto-dimension,' grinned Oli, and as he climbed back into bed he was hit on the head by a rugby ball.

Daisy was so startled when the Great Hall door closed behind Tara that she clutched her suit of armour and nearly sent it crashing to the floor. She darted over to the door, put her ear against the wood and listened to the scuffle beyond, wondering nervously whether to intervene. Then she caught the words, '. . . lock you in the tower,' and realised with relief that it would be much better to stay hidden from Madam Moonbeam so that she could fetch the boys and they could make a rescue plan together. After a few moments of silence from within the Great Hall, she opened the door and peeped inside. The room was safely empty and Daisy was about to withdraw when she noticed, lying on a chair, the Spookoscope. She grabbed it and fled out of the room and up the stairs. Then she heard quick footsteps behind her and she just managed to dart round a corner before Madam Moonbeam swept past, heading for the stairs.

She's locked Tara in the tower and now she's going back down for the Spookoscope, thought Daisy. Sure enough, a short while later Madam Moonbeam came puffing slowly back up the stairs. She was frowning to herself and carrying the Gerald-projector. As Daisy watched she went to a nearby door and unlocked it, but surprisingly she did not go into that room but into another, a few doors further on. Daisy crept to the first door that Madam Moonbeam had unlocked. She took a deep breath and went inside.

Peering through the darkness, she could make out two four-poster beds, each with the bump of a body in it. But whose body? What if this was the Spiffings' bedroom? Daisy wound up her courage for a closer look and, as she tiptoed forwards, her foot touched something unexpected. She glanced down. The unexpected something was large and egg-shaped. Phew! Lord and Lady Spiffing would *never* have a rugby ball in their bedroom. Daisy ran over to the window to draw back the curtains and then shook the moonlit contents of the nearest bed. The bump surfaced and blinked.

'Daisy!' cried Oli. 'What are you doing here?'

'Oh, Oli! Thank goodness I've found you! It's terrible – she's taken Tara!'

'Who has?'

'Madam Moonbeam! She's locked her in the tower!'

Oli clambered down from his bed and went to shake the other bump. 'Skipjack! Wake up!'

Skipjack was always a reluctant waker but when he finally focused his bleary eyes on Daisy and saw what she was holding, he shot out of bed as if fired from a cannon.

'You've got it!' he cried, seizing the precious Spookoscope from Daisy and planting kisses all over it. 'Thank you, Daisy – you've saved me from *two* fates worse than death! You are my favourite person in the universe! Apart from the Captain of the All Blacks, that is.'

Daisy went a little pink and giggled.

Oli decided it was time to get on. 'Listen, Skip – Madam Moonbeam's kidnapped Tara. Tell us what happened, Daisy.'

Daisy stopped giggling and started telling. 'It all started when Tara and I found this in one of Granddad's catalogues,' she said, and from her pocket she took a torn sheet of paper which she unfolded and spread out for the boys to see.

'It's Gerald,' said Skipjack. 'What's he doing advertising video cameras?'

'So, Gerald came from a shop.' Oli nodded. 'We were right, Skip: Madam Moonbeam is definitely a fraud.'

'We came to warn you,' said Daisy. 'But then Tara got caught.'

'I wonder what she's up to – and whether Lord and Lady Spiffing are in on it,' said Skipjack.

'They can't be,' replied Oli, 'or Madam Moonbeam wouldn't have hidden Tara in the tower. She would have raised the alarm instead. The Spiffings must be paying her to make the ghosts appear and they don't realise she's just fobbing them off with tricks.'

'Perhaps she's after the treasure!' cried Skipjack. 'And she stole the Spookoscope to talk to Uncle Beetle herself and be the first to get to it!'

Daisy looked dismayed. 'Poor Lord and Lady Spiffing. Shall we tell them?'

'Not yet,' said Oli. 'It's better if Madam Moonbeam doesn't know we suspect her. Also, we haven't got any proof that she's a phoney.'

'What about the Gerald-projector?' asked Skipjack. 'That's proof.'

'She's just taken it,' Daisy told them.

'Oh, rats,' said Skipjack.

'In that case there's definitely no point in telling the Spiffings,' said Oli. 'They'd never believe she's a baddie, especially since Tara was the one who broke in.'

'Grown-ups always side with grown-ups,' sighed Skipjack. 'Even when it's completely obvious they're fibbing.'

'We need to think of a way to rescue Tara,' said Oli.

'And get our own back on horrible Madam Moonbeam,' added Daisy.

'Skip, we need one of your plans.'

Skipjack was pleased; this was the bit he was good at. He settled down to think.

When Skipjack thought, the one part of his

body that worked even harder than his brain was his face. He looked like a chimpanzee trying to remove by tongue several apple pips from his back teeth while seeing if a fly has landed on his forehead. Finally his face cleared into a broad grin. 'Got it,' he said.

'I saw a film once,' began Skipjack. 'Someone rescued his friend from a locked room by using a key that he'd found in another door. It was a really old house like this, you see, and in those days they were a bit useless at making keys so the same one would fit in lots of different locks.'

'I'm with you,' said Oli. 'We try different keys in the tower door lock and one of them might work.'

'Excellent, Oliver – have a gold star,' said Skipjack and Daisy giggled. 'Now, here comes the good bit. After we've rescued Tara, we quickly hide the Spookoscope in the bathroom, and then Daisy and Tara lock us in here again before they escape. So in the morning, Madam Moonbeam finds two things that freak her out: Tara has vanished and the Spookoscope has un-vanished.'

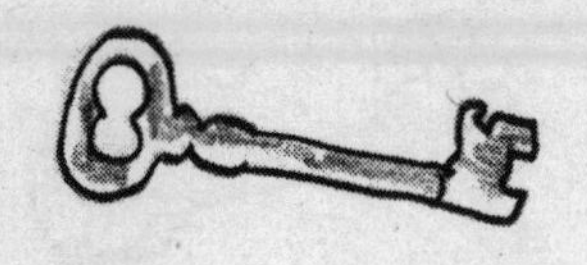

'And the Spiffings will go on thinking it was Uncle Beetle, and she won't be able to say it wasn't,' said Oli.

'And with any luck she'll think she's gone crazy,' finished Skipjack, 'and run away to Loony Land. So that's the plan. Get it?'

'Got it.'

'Good.'

Daisy giggled again. 'I think you're *really* clever to think of all that,' she said, and it was Skipjack's turn to go pink. He couldn't even remember the last time anyone had called him clever, apart from his mum, who didn't count.

Oli stuck his head out of their bedroom door.

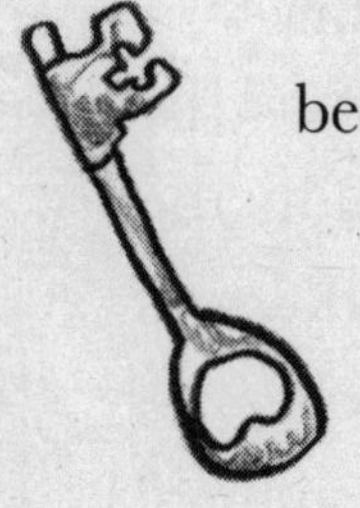

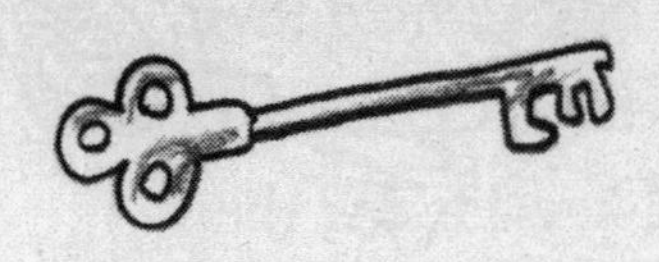 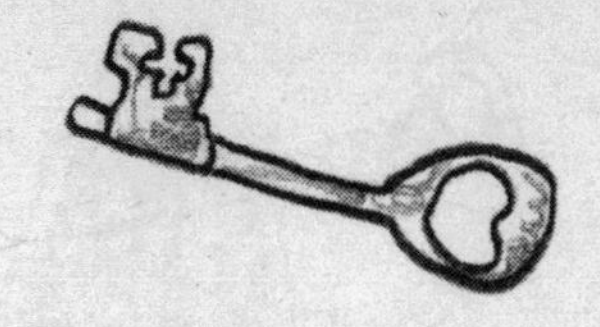

'All clear!' he whispered and they slipped out. Skipjack took their own key out of its keyhole and they collected several more from all the doors along the corridors. By the time they reached the tower door they were jangling like a posse of jailers doing the rounds of Wormwood Scrubs Prison.

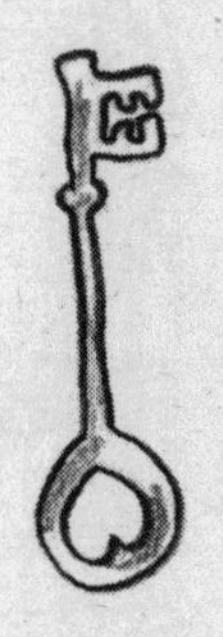

Oli tried all his keys in the lock, and then all those Daisy was holding and finally all of Skipjack's. But to everyone's annoyance, not one key would open the door.

'I'm going to write to the guy who made that film and complain,' grumbled Skipjack.

'Wait,' said Daisy suddenly and from her pocket she produced another key. 'Try this. It's from the back door.'

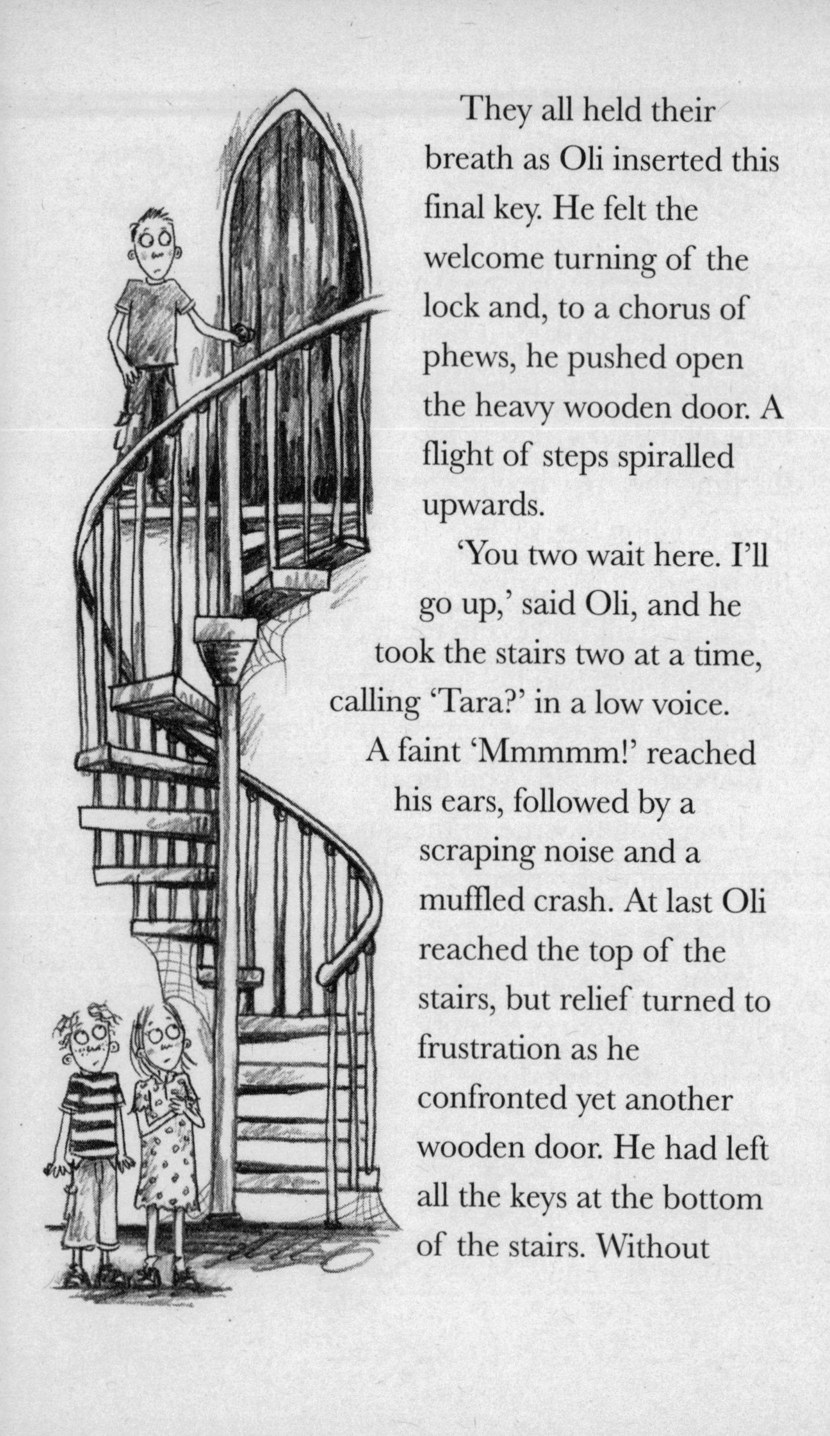

They all held their breath as Oli inserted this final key. He felt the welcome turning of the lock and, to a chorus of phews, he pushed open the heavy wooden door. A flight of steps spiralled upwards.

'You two wait here. I'll go up,' said Oli, and he took the stairs two at a time, calling 'Tara?' in a low voice. A faint 'Mmmmm!' reached his ears, followed by a scraping noise and a muffled crash. At last Oli reached the top of the stairs, but relief turned to frustration as he confronted yet another wooden door. He had left all the keys at the bottom of the stairs. Without much hope, he turned the handle and gave a quick push. The door opened.

'Tara!' He ran over to his sister. 'Are you OK?' She was lying on the floor, tied to a fallen chair.

'Mmmm!' she said impatiently. Oli ripped the tape from across her mouth.

'Ow!' she exclaimed. 'That hurt!'

'I'm *so* sorry, Your Ladyship,' replied Oli through clenched teeth. 'I'm in a bit of a hurry.'

He fumbled with the knots but his fingernails were too short to loosen them quickly so he took out his penknife instead. Tara saw the moonlit gleam of the blade and tried to shuffle away.

'Keep still or you'll be stabbed!' muttered Oli and for once, she did not argue. Oli sawed at the purple cord until at last it fell in snakes on the floor.

'Finally!' Tara leapt to her feet and ran to the door. She turned to see why Oli was not following her and saw that he was carefully picking up every last thread of cord. 'What *are* you doing?' she demanded.

'It's called getting rid of the evidence,' said her brother.

'Why?' asked Tara.

'No time to explain.'

They ran back down the spiral staircase to where the others still waited. Daisy locked the door after them, pocketing the key, and as they tiptoed back through the silent castle they slipped a key into each of the locks they passed.

'They'll all be in the wrong doors now,' giggled Daisy, 'but the Spiffings will just blame Uncle Beetle.'

When they reached the boys' room, Oli took up the Spookoscope and nipped out with it.

'Where's he going?' demanded Tara.

'He's hiding it in the bathroom,' explained Skipjack.

'Why?'

'No time to explain.'

Oli reappeared. 'Now, lock us in,' he said to the girls, 'and make sure you leave the key in the lock. Good luck.' He closed the door and they heard the key turn, Tara whisper, 'Why?' and then silence.

Violet Moonbeam was not a morning person. So when she was jolted awake by thuds and crashes and saw from her bedside clock that it was only half past seven, she was not a happy bunny. At first she thought the noises were inside her head, which had ached terribly all night with worry. She was only trying to earn a bit of money and make two old people happy, and now suddenly she was a kidnapper! But as the thuds and crashes continued, Violet Moonbeam realised they were not coming from inside her head after all, or even inside her room, but from somewhere down the corridor.

'Help!' a voice was calling. 'Someone rescue us!'

She heard a polite knock. 'Are you all right in there?' enquired Lord Spiffing.

'We've been locked in!' called the boys. 'Can you let us out, please?'

'Yes, I can. The key's right here.' Lord Spiffing turned it and opened the door. He blinked at the boys, as if surprised to find them on the other side. 'Hello, hello,' he said. 'What are you two doing here?'

'This is our bedroom,' explained Oli.

'How very odd. Ah-ha – good morning Madam Moonbeam,' said Lord Spiffing as the clairvoyant emerged from her room.

'Extraordinary thing – these two boys were locked in their room last night. I wonder how that could have happened.'

'Do you wonder, too, Madam Moonbeam?' asked Skipjack, wide-eyed.

Violet Moonbeam did indeed wonder how the door had become locked again after she herself had unlocked it on her way back to her room. She decided that in her haste she couldn't have turned the key fully.

'I had another message from Great-Uncle Bartholomew,' she whispered, 'saying it was him. The rest of your Dear Departed suspected these boys might try to find their wicked contraption in the night. They begged him to do something.'

'Well, you can tell him from me that my Dear Departed are getting a bit big for their boots,' commented Lord Spiffing.

'Perhaps you should be grateful to them, Lord Spiffing,' said Madam Moonbeam. 'After all, last night they sent me a psychic warning that there was an intruder in the house.'

'No, no,' said Lord Spiffing confidently, and the subject of psychic warnings was not one he usually felt confident about. 'No, that was the dogs. I went to check and there was no one about. It must have been mice again.'

'I assure you there was someone about. It was –' and here she used the old theatre trick of counting to three to create maximum suspense – 'a girl.'

'A girl?' cried Lord Spiffing. 'Well, I'm jiggered!'

Oli and Skipjack exchanged glances. This would be interesting.

'The spirits led me to the Great Hall,' continued Madam Moonbeam, 'where they helped me to capture her. She is at present locked in the tower.'

Lord Spiffing was so shocked he completely lost control of his eyebrows. 'Good grief! Shall we call the police?' Then another idea struck him and he asked hopefully, 'Shall I take along my Viking battle-axe?'

'Oh, no, Your Lordship,' said Madam Moonbeam. 'I think a stern word will be punishment enough.'

'A stern word,' nodded Lord Spiffing. 'Right-oh.' And they all set off to the tower, where Madam Moonbeam took a large iron key from her pocket to unlock the door. 'She's in the room at the top,' she whispered.

Oli had to elbow Skipjack several times on the way up the spiral staircase to stop him giggling.

The bare little room was, of course, empty.

Violet Moonbeam couldn't have looked more shocked if Uncle Beetle had been there, juggling bananas with his underpants on his head.

'This is impossible!' she cried. Then a thought seemed to go 'ting!' inside her head and she turned to fix a beady eye on Oli and Skipjack.

But when you have faced the bone-crushing Slugger Stubbins in a scrum-down and the rage of demon bus driver Mr Albert Grimble, you are more than equal to a beady from Madam Moonbeam. Both boys met her glare with their fearless 'Who, us?' look.

Lord Spiffing gave her a friendly pat on the back. 'Poor Madam Moonbeam. Perhaps you dreamt it all. Or else it was one of my nincompoop ancestors playing a trick on you. Come and have some breakfast.'

What Violet Moonbeam wanted to say now was that she would rather share a bowl of pickled rats' eyeballs with Fungus the Bogeyman than have breakfast with the sniggering, nudging Oli and Skipjack. What she in fact said was, 'Thank you, Lord Spiffing, but I think I'll go and have a lie-down.'

A little later, while the boys were tucking into porridge with cream and brown sugar, Skipjack asked, as casually as possible, 'Did you ever have a relation called Norman?'

Both Spiffings stopped eating at once and exchanged uncomfortable glances.

'You did, then,' said Skipjack. 'What was he like?'

There was a long pause before Lord Spiffing said, 'Poor Norman was a cousin of mine who used to spend his holidays here. He was a very odd boy.'

'In what way?' asked Oli.

'To start with, he was much too clever.'

'Is that odd?'

'It is in my family,' Lord Spiffing assured him. 'Extremely odd. But he was also very mean. And smelly. None of us ever wanted to play with him. We all teased him and laughed at him – I feel rather bad about that now. Anyhow, as the years went by he became odder and odder. Finally –'

He stopped and frowned at his wife.

'You'd better tell the whole story, Algy,' she said, 'just in case they see him through the magic hat.'

Lord Spiffing sighed. 'Very well. Finally it occurred to us that Norman was always at his very oddest during a full moon. He'd take himself off for long walks in the middle of the night and come back all scratched and cut with his clothes torn. Well of course, lots of people go a bit crackers under a full moon – my cow Mildred for instance becomes very excitable. But this was different. So we called in a brain doctor chap who did some tests and he told us what was wrong with Norman. You'll never guess.'

Skipjack had been sinking lower and lower in his chair with every detail of this story, as if fear was dissolving his bones. 'What will we never guess?' he croaked.

Lord Spiffing, who was now pacing the room in agitation, stopped and took a deep breath. 'Cousin Norman was a *werewolf*!'

Skipjack slid to the floor with a clatter.

'Is he all right?' asked Lady Spiffing anxiously peering under the table.

'He doesn't like werewolves,' explained Oli, hauling his friend back up.

'Who does?' agreed Lord Spiffing. 'We had to lock Norman in the cellar every time there was a full moon so he couldn't go charging around the countryside frightening the sheep and being a nuisance to everybody.'

'Did he die in the cellar?' asked Oli.

'No, at the vet's. He caught dog flu.'

'That was forty years ago,' said Lady Spiffing, 'And to this day none of our dogs will go near that cellar. It's the one in the hall. We put a sign on the door saying "dungeon" because dungeons are more touristy.'

'What a lot of eggs you collected today, Binky,' commented Lord Spiffing, glancing into a basket on the dresser. 'We must have some for lunch, on our hash.'

'The hens always seem to lay more,' remarked his wife, 'when there's a full moon.'

Skipjack gasped. 'You don't mean there's a f-f-full moon tonight?'

'There must be,' said Lord Spiffing. 'Look at all those eggs.'

Skipjack's porridge with cream and brown sugar had turned to ashes in his mouth. He pushed his bowl away with a sigh. 'I'm sorry,' he said. 'I'm not very hungry this morning.'

Lady Spiffing patted his hand. 'Now, you mustn't worry,' she said kindly. 'We'll find your magic hat.'

'Come on, Skip, let's go and start looking,' said Oli, dragging his boneless friend to his feet.

'Just when I thought things couldn't get any worse,' moaned Skipjack as Oli steered him out of the kitchen, 'they get even worse than worse!'

'So, Norman's plan is really to turn Lord

Spiffing into a werewolf,' said Oli thoughtfully.

'And if he doesn't succeed, he'll turn *me* into a werewolf!' Skipjack wailed.

'I don't think he can do that, cos he didn't manage to get right into your head. All the same, it won't be very nice being haunted by him during the full moon. He's bound to get much smellier and howl a lot. We've just got to make even more sure we offload him to Lord Spiffing before this evening's deadline.'

Skipjack shuddered. 'Please don't use the word *dead*.' Then he stopped and sniffed the air. 'He's coming,' he groaned. 'I can smell him. And I'm on my own again, cos the Spookoscope's upstairs.'

'Remember he's only a ghost,' whispered Oli. 'Don't let him scare you.'

'I won't,' said Skipjack and clenched his teeth.

'So, you've found out my secret,' hissed Norman.

'Yes,' squeaked Skipjack.

'I hope you're going to try even harder now to help me.'

'Yes,' squeaked Skipjack.

'You're not very chatty this morning. What's the matter – scared?'

'Yes,' squeaked Skipjack.

'Not half as scared as you will be by nightfall tonight,' whispered Norman. 'See you then.'

'Has he gone?' asked Oli.

'Yes,' squeaked Skipjack.

'Can you stop squeaking now?'

'No,' squeaked Skipjack.

Oli gave his friend a comforting thump. 'Stay cool, Skip. Lord Spiffing is bursting to try on the Spookoscope. You'll be Norman-free long before werewolf time, I promise.'

'Well, come on then,' said Skipjack. 'Let's get it right now and give it to him.'

'We have to pretend to search for it first,' Oli reminded him. 'It'll look suspicious if we find it too quickly.'

They spent the next ten minutes hanging around the castle bathrooms and calling to one another, 'Have you found it yet?' and, 'It's not here – where can that naughty Uncle Beetle have hidden it?'

Downstairs in the drawing room, meanwhile, Violet Moonbeam was busy with the Ghost of the Blue Lady. Keen to produce something truly spectacular to replace Gerald and to score some points with the Spiffings, she was rigging up her most expensive special effect – a whoosh of blue smoke with a blood-curdling wail.

The Mystery of the Disappearing Prisoner was still stretching her brain cells. She longed to blame the boys but she couldn't explain the two locked doors. Only ghosts could pass through locked doors. Violet Moonbeam may not have known much about ghosts, but she was fairly sure they didn't come like Oli and Skipjack. And, having carried the girl all the way up to the tower, Violet Moonbeam would have sworn that she was solid, too. So how had she escaped? And how had the dratted contraption disappeared from the Great Hall?

Madam Moonbeam's tangled thoughts were interrupted by a yell of 'FOUND IT!' followed by a sound like a large herd of wildebeest, apparently migrating down the stairs. Madam Moonbeam put her eye to the drawing-room

keyhole and saw Oli and Skipjack standing at the foot of the stairs, triumphantly waving the Spookoscope.

'We found it in a bathroom,' Oli was explaining to the delighted Spiffings. 'So it must have been Uncle Beetle, just like Madam Moonbeam said.'

'Madam Moonbeam is amazing with ghosts,' shouted Skipjack in the direction of the drawing-room door. 'She is definitely a real psycho.'

'Psychic,' corrected Oli. 'Psycho is the other one.'

'Splendid, splendid,' beamed Lord Spiffing. 'Come along all – to the library! We won't interrupt Madam Moonbeam. She doesn't much care for the magic hat in any case.'

Violet Moonbeam straightened herself, gripping the door handle for support. Her head was spinning. Was it possible that Great-Uncle Bartholomew's ghost had taken the dratted contraption from the Great Hall and hidden it in the bathroom, just to serve her right? Or was she – gulp – *really* psychic?

When everyone – except the magnificently muddled Madam Moonbeam – was assembled in the library, Oli donned the Spookoscope once more and looked all around. At first the room seemed ghost-free but then a voice behind him said, 'Boo!'

'Argh!' Oli spun round and came face to misty face with Uncle Beetle.

'I say – are you all right?' asked Lord Spiffing.

'You gave me a shock!' exclaimed Oli.

'I'm terribly sorry,' said Lord Spiffing.

'I only said "Boo",' objected Uncle Beetle. 'That's what ghosts are supposed to do. I could have been much scarier and done all that "wooooooooooo" business.'

'You were scary enough,' grumbled Oli.

'I do apologise,' said Lord Spiffing. 'Can you see him yet?'

'Yes – he's right here.'

'Splendid, splendid. Ask him about the treasure.'

'You can ask him yourself, Lord Spiffing,' said Oli. 'He can hear you perfectly well.'

'Yes, I suppose he can. Well, here goes.' Lord Spiffing cleared his throat and began to speak, in capital letters as though to someone old, deaf and foreign.

'CAN – YOU – TELL – ME – WHERE – YOU – HAVE – HIDDEN – THE – TREASURE?' he shouted.

Uncle Beetle flew across the library, put his nose right up to Lord Spiffing's and bellowed, 'NO!'

'He says no,' said Oli, coughing a lot to try to stop himself laughing.

'WHY – NOT!' shouted Lord Spiffing. Then he turned to Oli and exclaimed, 'This is silly. Why don't I simply talk to him myself?' He held his hand out for the Spookoscope.

Skipjack gulped. This was it – the longed-for

moment when his own personal Norman siege could be lifted. He should feel as light as a balloon on the moon, but instead he felt like the rope in a tug of war. Guilt was pulling him in one direction, saying, 'You cannot impose Norman on a rugby-playing, ketchup-eating dude like Lord Spiffing.' At the same time Self-Preservation was pulling him in the opposite direction, arguing, 'This will be your last chance.' Finally Norman himself came in at S-P's end, hissing, 'Do it, NOW!'

Skipjack nodded to Oli, who peeled off the Spookoscope and handed it over to the doomed Lord Spiffing.

'Thank you. This is very exciting, I must say,' chattered His Lordship as he fastened the chinstrap, happily unaware of the heavy blow that was about to strike him. 'Now, where's that Beetle?' He squinted through the goggles. 'I can't see him. I can't see any ghosts at all,' he complained. He looked down at the control box in his right hand. 'What happens if I turn this?' he asked, and he pinched the Psychic Surge button between his finger and thumb.

'STOP!'

It was Skipjack. 'Don't touch that red button!' he shouted. Then he turned to give Oli a look of pure despair before sinking on to the sofa with his head in his hands. 'I couldn't let him do it,' he mumbled.

'Do what?' asked Lord Spiffing.

Oli crouched down next to his friend and gave him a pat. 'You were quite right, Skip. We'll find another way.'

'Will somebody please tell me what's going on?' demanded Lord Spiffing, raising his goggles.

'I'm being haunted,' sighed Skipjack. 'By your cousin Norman.'

Lord Spiffing was so shocked by this news that his eyebrows nearly left his forehead altogether to shoot into outer space. 'Well, I'm jiggered!'

'It's you he's really after,' said Oli. 'He wanted Skipjack to get you to put on the Spookoscope before nightfall tonight. He was going to use it to get inside your head.'

Lord Spiffing hurriedly pulled off the dangerous article. 'Is he in my head now?'

'No, because Skipjack stopped you before you turned up the Psychic Surge button,' explained Oli.

'I'm most terribly grateful,' said Lord Spiffing, taking out a large spotted handkerchief and giving his brow a mop. 'But, does that mean he's in *your* head? We did mention that he was, er, a werewolf?'

'Yes, you did. That was the moment I slid under the table, remember?' said Skipjack, who was still feeling sore. 'He's not quite in my head – he just pops up whenever he feels like a good haunt. He says if he can't get inside your head, he'll stick around me for the rest of my life.'

'What a meanie,' put in Lady Spiffing, shaking her head. 'No wonder you never wanted to play with him, Algy.'

Lord Spiffing was frowning. 'I can't let you be haunted by Cousin Norman for the rest of your life,' he said. 'It would be most unfair. Wouldn't it, Binky?'

'Most unfair,' agreed Lady Spiffing. 'But what is one to do?'

Lord Spiffing drew himself up. There was only one thing that a man with Viking blood in his veins could do, and that was the Brave Thing. 'It's quite simple, my dear,' he said in a firm voice. 'If we can't think of another solution by nightfall, I will put on the magic hat again and turn that red button.'

Skipjack sat up and gazed at Lord Spiffing in wonder. The man was nothing short of a hero. 'Thank you, sir,' he mumbled.

'Will you turn into a werewolf, Algy?' enquired Lady Spiffing.

'Just for one night a month,' explained her husband, 'When there's a full moon. We can cope with that, can't we, Binky?'

'It'll be like having another dog,' mused Lady Spiffing. 'Except I might not let you sleep on the bed.'

'Meanwhile,' said Lord Spiffing, passing the Spookoscope back to Oli, 'let's see whether you can get anything out of old Beetle. If I'm going to be a werewolf I could at least be a rich werewolf.'

As Oli put the Spookoscope on once more, Madam Moonbeam arrived on the scene, drawn by curiosity and the desire to test her psychic skills. 'The spirits have begged me to be present to protect them from the wicked contraption,' she announced. 'I see I have arrived just in time.'

'It's very kind of you to assist them,' said Lady Spiffing graciously. 'Do sit down.'

Oli scanned the room for Uncle Beetle. Then he burst out laughing.

Madam Moonbeam gave a short, sharp sigh. 'All right, where is he now?'

'He's on your lap,' chuckled Oli, 'with his arms round you, blowing kisses.'

Violet Moonbeam leapt up with a shriek, sending her lap-ghost flying into the air.

'That is the limit!' she screeched. 'I will not be ridiculed by some fool who's been dead for a hundred years.' She thundered towards Oli like a member of that rare and dangerous species, *rhinoceros furious*. 'I'm going to give that Bartholomew a piece of my mind,' she muttered as she yanked off the Spookoscope and rammed it down on her own head. Then she fumbled for the control box at the end of its long wire and, ignoring shouts of 'DON'T!' from all around, she turned the Psychic Surge button to High.

There followed a buzzing noise and a strong

smell of burnt rubber. A fizzle of sparks shot out of the Spookoscope. Madam Moonbeam dropped the control box and stood, frozen in a trance.

Oli, who was standing very close to her, felt stunned and dizzy. To his amazement he could still see Uncle Beetle, even without the Spookoscope. The ghost had flown to the top of one of the bookcases, but something extraordinary was happening to him.

Like a cobweb sucked up by a vacuum cleaner, Uncle Beetle was being pulled towards Madam Moonbeam.

'What's going on?' demanded Skipjack, seeing Oli's astonished face.

'Uncle Beetle's trying to hold on to the bookcase,' said Oli. 'But his feet have disappeared up Madam Moonbeam's nose.'

'Nooooooo!' shouted the ghost, but he went on stretching, longer and longer. Finally he could cling on no more; his fingers slipped from the bookcase and he went pinging into Madam Moonbeam, who gave an enormous sniff, swallowed and burped.

Violet Moonbeam blinked a few times, but when she opened her mouth to speak it was not with her own voice.

'Will somebody get me out of here?' shouted Great-Uncle Bartholomew.

'Uncle Beetle? gasped Lord Spiffing. 'Is that you in there?'

'Of course it's me. Who did you think it was, Queen Victoria? This dreadful woman's gone and swallowed me up. I demand that someone get me out this instant.'

'What *are* we going to do?' giggled Lady Spiffing, trying to look suitably shocked.

Oli had an idea but he was not ready to come to the rescue until Uncle Beetle had agreed to a deal.

'We'll only help you,' he said, 'if you tell Lord and Lady Spiffing where your treasure is.'

Uncle Beetle flung Madam Moonbeam's arms up in annoyance. 'But that will put an end to all my fun!' he shouted.

Oli shrugged. 'OK,' he said. 'In that case, we'll leave you where you are.'

'Wait! It does smell revolting in here,' muttered the ghost. 'Herbal tea and cheap lavender soap. I'm not sure how long I can stand it. All right, you spoilsports – I shall give you a little clue. And if you're too bone-headed to work it out, you don't deserve to find the treasure. How's that?'

Lord Spiffing nodded. 'I've always been very good at clues,' he declared. 'Years of crossword puzzles and detective stories. Come on, Uncle Beetle, let's have it.'

'You will find the clue,' came the reply, 'on my behind.'

'Is that it?' asked Lord Spiffing.

'That's it. Now, I've kept my end of the bargain. Kindly get me out of this horrible purple prison.'

Oli picked up the control box from the floor and turned the Psychic Surge button off again.

'Hooray.' Uncle Beetle began to squeeze out of Madam Moonbeam's left ear. 'That experience will haunt me for ever,' he shuddered. 'Pip-pip.' Oli watched him fly into the furthest possible corner of the room and slowly fade away. Madam Moonbeam crumpled on to the floor in a dead faint

'Poor Madam Moonbeam,' said Lady Spiffing. 'I'll get her a cushion.'

'It's a shame she didn't suck Norman up while she was at it,' remarked Skipjack. 'He might have decided to stay there and our problems would have been solved.'

'No chance,' he heard Norman mutter. 'I'm not that desperate.'

'What about that clue, eh?' wondered Lord Spiffing. '"You'll find the clue on my behind."'

'It's a shame he left before we could ask him to bend over,' said Skipjack. 'He might have a tattoo on his bottom.'

'My ancestors,' said His Lordship stiffly, 'do not have tattoos on their bottoms.'

'Perhaps he meant behind a picture of him, or a photograph or something?' suggested Oli.

'Let's look on the back of his portrait.'

This idea was greeted with enthusiasm and Uncle Beetle's portrait was at once taken down. At first no one could see anything at all like a clue on the brown paper backing, but then Skipjack's sharp eyes noticed some faint marks in one corner.

'They look a bit like hieroglyphics,' said Oli.

'Ah-ha. Uncle Beetle would have been a dab hand at those,' Lord Spiffing told them, 'because he spent so much time in Egypt.'

'What we need is a list of hieroglyphics and their translations,' said his wife. 'Where's that old book on Egypt?'

'It should be here somewhere,' replied Lord Spiffing, waving an arm at the shelves of books which lined the walls. 'Come on, everybody – it's big and red.'

They all took a section of the library and began searching. After a few moments Lord Spiffing exclaimed, 'Ah-ha!'

'Have you found it?' asked his wife.

'No, but I've found a copy of *Liver Disease and the Jersey Cow* which I've been looking for since

May. Now, if I could only find that book on winter feeding problems I'd be a happy man.'

'Got it!' called Oli.

'Clever lad,' said Lord Spiffing, pleased. 'Mildred caused me a lot of anxiety last year by going off her hay.'

'Not the cow book, Algy,' sighed his wife. 'The Egypt book.'

Oli laid the large crimson book on a desk and Lord Spiffing turned the yellowed pages, past pictures of pharaohs, pyramids and mummies, until he came to several columns of beautifully drawn picture-letters with their modern equivalents. He peered closely up and down the page. 'I can't see a thing without my specs,' he remarked. 'You

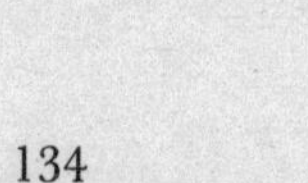

boys will have to decode for us.'

'OK,' said Oli. 'Skip, tell me what comes first.'

Skipjack squinted at the back of the portrait. 'A bird?' he said doubtfully.

Oli looked down the columns and quickly found their first problem. 'Half these letters look like birds, Skip. What kind of bird is it?'

'I dunno – Just a bird,' said Skipjack, who could hardly have told a duck from a dodo.

'It's rather a sweet little bird,' remarked Lady Spiffing over his shoulder. 'It looks like a fluffy baby chick.'

'Found it,' said Oli. 'It's an *oo*. Next?'

'Next is a square,' said Skipjack with much

more confidence. Squares he could do.

'Got it. That's a *p*. After that?'

'A worm.'

'A worm?'

'A worm.' Skipjack was at the top of his game now, worms being a particular field of expertise.

'OK, that's an *n*,' said Oli.

'The next shape is a bit like another square but the lines don't meet,' said Lady Spiffing.

'I think that's *h*,' reported Oli.

'And then there's the one that looks like a knife standing upright,' said Skipjack.

'Found that. It's *ee* or *y*.'

'The last one is a UFO.'

'A UFO?' repeated Oli in disbelief. 'There aren't any UFOs on my list.'

'It's definitely a UFO,' agreed Lady Spiffing. 'A proper flying saucer.'

'Or a squashed rugby ball,' suggested Skipjack.

'Well, why didn't you say so?' said Oli. 'That's easy. It's an *r*.'

'And that's all,' said Skipjack. 'So, what have we got?'

‘*Oopnhyr*,’ Oli told him.

‘*Oopnhyr*? That’s more like Welsh than Egyptian,’ commented Lady Spiffing. ‘Or possibly Dutch.’

Lord Spiffing was about to express his dismay at having to learn the two most impossible languages in Europe to find the treasure when, for the second time that day, Skipjack came to his rescue.

'I know what it means!' he cried, with a sudden flash of insight. 'It's not Welsh or Dutch – it just means "open here", like on a packet of chocolate chip cookies!'

'Ah-ha!' Lord Spiffing beamed, relieved. 'Thank heavens for that. So the treasure must be hidden inside this very portrait.'

'It must be rather flat treasure,' remarked his wife.

'We need a knife,' said Lord Spiffing, 'to cut the brown paper.'

'I've got a penknife,' said Oli. 'Here you are.'

Everyone leaned in to watch as Lord Spiffing carefully cut round three sides of the brown paper and lifted it back. Taped to the frame beneath was a white card covered in spidery black handwriting. Lord Spiffing took one look at it, said, 'Squiggles again,' and handed it to Oli.

Oli deciphered it with difficulty. 'To Beetle Spiffing,' he read, 'a fiendishly good card player, I give my Golden Scarab of Amenhotep III, in payment for losing at Snap. Signed: General Gordon.'

'Well, I'm jiggered,' breathed Lord Spiffing. 'A golden scarab! So that's what the treasure is. We just need to look for a golden scarab. What is a scarab, anyway?'

'It's a beetle, Algy,' said Lady Spiffing. 'An ancient Egyptian beetle.'

'But there are heaps and heaps of beetles in this castle,' objected Lord Spiffing. 'How on earth do we find the one that will pay for the roof?'

'Well, it has to be golden for a start,' said Oli. 'You can't have many golden beetles, surely?'

'I don't think we've got one. Anything golden we had was sold long ago.'

'What about the big yellow door stopper in our bedroom?' suggested Skipjack. 'The one I keep stubbing my toe on. That looks a bit beetly.

Perhaps that's the Golden Scarab of I'm In Hot Water or whatever he's called.'

Lord Spiffing shook his head. 'Oh, no, my boy. That's just a nasty concrete souvenir. It's not worth a bag of beans.'

There was a pause and then the Spiffings exchanged glances which were clearly labelled with the unspoken question, 'Or is it?'

'Come along, all!' shouted Lord Spiffing. 'To the Egyptian room!'

So, leaving Madam Moonbeam still snoring on the library floor, they all galloped up to Oli and Skipjack's bedroom. Here, closer inspection of the nasty concrete souvenir revealed that it was indeed made of solid gold. Lady Spiffing at once took the doorstop away from the dusty floor to polish it up, while her husband, very jiggered indeed, made a phone call to the British Museum.

'I spoke to an Expert who sounded very interested,' he reported a short while later to the others in the kitchen. 'He says that if it's genuine it'll be worth thousands. We should be able to get the roof mended and still have change to buy some company for Mildred.' He beamed. 'I think that calls for some lunch, don't you?'

The mention of food reminded Skipjack that he had left most of his porridge uneaten at breakfast. Now that Lord Spiffing had volunteered to relieve him of Norman before nightfall, Skipjack's worries had flown away and his appetite came stampeding back. 'Good idea,' he said. 'All that treasure-hunting has made me hungry.'

'Corned beef hash with a fried egg on top?'

'Yummy.'

While Lord Spiffing got busy with the frying pan and his wife went to see whether Madam Moonbeam had woken up yet, the boys were sent to the shed with a basket to fetch a load of wood for the stove. During their expedition they discussed the happy outcome of the treasure hunt and Skipjack said, 'I wish we could think of another way of dealing with Norman.'

'I don't suppose we could get him inside Madam Moonbeam?' suggested Oli as he pushed open the kitchen door for Skipjack and the pile of wood.

'I doubt it,' replied Skipjack, dropping the basket beside the cooking range. 'Even if we could persuade Norman to go up her nose instead of Lord Spiffing's, we'd never get the old cow to put on the Spookoscope again.'

Lord Spiffing's wooden spoon ground to a halt in the pan and he muttered awkwardly, 'I know you're trying to help, boys, but I couldn't stand to see her suffer.'

'I'm sorry,' said Oli. 'I didn't know you were so fond of her.'

'Fond of her? She's the most precious thing in the world to me. Apart from my wife, of course.'

'Anyway, she'd never agree to it,' said Skipjack gloomily.

'We'd have a bit of trouble getting the magic hat on,' agreed Lord Spiffing. 'She doesn't even like it when I clean her ears.'

'Clean her ears?'

'And she positively hates having her hoofs done.'

At this perplexing point, Lady Spiffing returned from the library with the Spookoscope and the news flash that Madam Moonbeam was now back in her bedroom, recovering from her ordeal.

'Binky, my dear,' said Lord Spiffing, 'the boys have just suggested getting Norman inside Mildred instead of me, but it seems rather mean on the old girl.'

'Not Mildred,' exclaimed Oli. 'Madam Moonbeam!'

Lord Spiffing looked blank. 'But I was talking about Mildred.'

'You are always talking about Mildred,' said his wife. 'As it happens, I think it's rather a good notion. I wouldn't have minded Norman once a month but now that I've seen what happened to Madam Moonbeam when Beetle went up her nose I'm having second thoughts.'

'It did look rather uncomfortable,' agreed Lord Spiffing thoughtfully.

'Given the choice,' she continued, 'I'd rather

have a were-cow than a were-husband. Anyway, Mildred might rather enjoy the chance to kick her heels up every four weeks and have a good gallop.'

This was not an aspect Lord Spiffing had considered and he could see that for a cow of Mildred's undoubted intelligence, a good gallop might make a nice change from standing about in a field all day with nothing to do but chew. Skipjack, however, was extremely doubtful that Norman would agree.

'Why don't we ask him?' suggested Lord Spiffing. 'Is he here now, or can you whistle for him?'

'You don't need to whistle,' said Norman suddenly, making Skipjack jump. 'I'm here.'

'Why don't you smell?' cried Skipjack.

Lord Spiffing looked hurt. 'Because I washed this morning.'

'You must be getting used to me, which is just as well at this rate,' said Norman.

'I'll never get used to you,' said Skipjack glumly.

Lord Spiffing nodded. 'That's what Agatha still says. Even after thirty years of marriage.'

'I'm not going inside the cow,' announced Norman.

By this time Oli had pulled on the Spookoscope and was able to repeat Norman's end of Skipjack's apparently random monologue to the Spiffings.

'It's Norman. He says he hasn't waited all this time to be solid again, only to be fobbed off with Mildred. He says he wants revenge.'

'Well, tell him not to be such a nincompoop,'

said His Lordship. 'I'll tell him myself. Don't be such a nincompoop, Norman. Revenge isn't going to keep you happy for ever, not in my dull old head anyway. Mildred is much more interesting than me.'

'Norman says you can't imagine how much interest he can get from revenge.' Oli told them.

'What if I say sorry for teasing you all those years ago?' said Lord Spiffing. 'Here goes: It was jolly mean of me and I'm very sorry. Will you forgive me?'

'Is he sorry,' asked Norman, 'for calling me Bog-rat and telling all the girls that I crawled out of a troll's armpit?'

When Oli repeated this Lady Spiffing exclaimed, 'Algy! You didn't!'

Her husband looked ashamed. 'I'm afraid I did. Yes, I'm very sorry for that, too,' he sighed.

'There you are, Norman,' said Lady Spiffing. 'He's very sorry. So won't you let bygones be bygones and pop into Mildred's head like a good ghost?'

'No,' said Norman and Oli shook his head for the Spiffings.

'Not even,' asked Skipjack, 'for a Scooby Snack?'

'No!' barked Norman. 'And you can't make me, so there!'

This angry outburst was followed by silence. 'I think he's gone,' said Oli.

'Oh, well,' sighed His Lordship. 'He's sure to change his mind before this evening. Let's have lunch.'

After double helpings of Spiffing Hash, this time with fried eggs on top, the boys wandered outside to while away the afternoon in the castle grounds. By a sort of unspoken agreement, neither mentioned Norman and they spent a happy hour exploring the gardens and woods before finishing up by the lake. Tied to a rickety jetty they found, to their delight, an old rowing boat complete with oars. Soon they were floating in the middle of the lake, each lying along a seat and gazing up at the blue sky. There was only one topic of conversation profound enough for such a perfect situation.

'Let's pick our dream teams,' said Oli happily. 'We'll start with rugby, and then do football and cricket.'

* * *

By the time the boys returned to the castle, the afternoon shadows had begun to lengthen. They found the Spiffings in one of the outbuildings, spreading the cobbled floor thickly with straw.

'Just in case Norman doesn't change his mind about Mildred,' puffed Lady Spiffing, we're going to lock Algy in here for the night.'

Let's go and have a cup of tea while we wait for the old bog-rat to come back,' said Lord Spiffing.

As they sat round the kitchen table a little while later, Oli and Skipjack marvelled at the sheer coolness of Lord Spiffing, who drank his tea and ate his fruit cake exactly like someone who was *not* about to turn into a werewolf.

All of a sudden Skipjack found himself wrapped in the old familiar stink. 'I knew I wouldn't get used to him!' he gasped, holding his nose. Then he listened for a moment and said, 'Norman wants everyone to know that the old bog-rat hasn't changed his mind.'

Lord Spiffing turned slightly pink. 'Well, he

shouldn't listen to other people's conversations,' he declared.

Lady Spiffing clicked her tongue. 'I think you are making a serious mistake, Norman,' she said. 'I really do. As long as you are stuck outside Skipjack like this, you can't scare anyone except Skipjack, which isn't much cop after forty years of being all alone. If Algy lets you into his head no one will notice much, as everyone thinks he's barmy anyway – I'm sorry, Algy, but they do. However, just think what fun you could have, Norman dear, as a haunted cow?'

'That's true!' exclaimed Lord Spiffing. 'People will come from miles around to be frightened by you.'

'You'll be a star, Norman,' said Oli. 'You'll be the most famous ghost in the world!'

'No one will ever call you bog-rat again,' said Skipjack. 'Or say you crawled out of a troll's armpit. You will be Awesome.'

There was a pause, and then there was another pause, and then Norman said, 'All right. I'll do it.'

The ten-acre field that had lain below the castle for a thousand years had been the scene of many an exciting event, from the epic Battle of Saxons' Wallop in 1089 to Herbert Haystack's record-breaking throw in Toss the Turnip at last year's Summer Fair. But even though its every clod was pickled in history, the field had remained, most visitors would agree, the least spooky part of Spiffing Castle.

That was about to change.

All the players had assembled: Oli (Guardian of the Spookoscope), Skipjack (Hopeful Norman-Disposer), Lord Spiffing (Cow-Handler) and Lady Spiffing (Official Observer). His Lordship made a gentle cooing noise and the star of the show trotted up. Mildred was a dainty, honey-coloured cow with slow-moving jaws and a rather vacant expression in her big brown eyes. Signs of the superior intelligence promised by Lord Spiffing were hard to locate and Oli hoped that Norman would not notice this too and call the whole operation off.

'Is Norman still here?' he asked Skipjack.

'Yes. He keeps saying "Hurry up". I think he's pacing around, cos the smell keeps moving. He seems a bit agitated.'

'He's probably nervous,' said Oli.

Lord Spiffing placed the Spookoscope on Mildred's head and fastened the strap. She looked surprised but made no objection.

'Ready?' asked Oli.

'Ready, Norman?' asked Skipjack.

'Ready,' said Norman. 'Get a move on.'

'Ready, Oli,' said Skipjack.

'Here goes,' said Oli and he turned the Psychic Surge button up to high.

The Spookoscope fizzled and sparked. Mildred looked more surprised. She even stopped chewing.

'Here I go!' yelled Norman.

Skipjack felt his left ear go pop. Mildred

snuffled and blinked a few times and then returned to her chewing. Oli removed the Spookoscope.

'Norman?' asked Skipjack nervously. 'Where are you?'

'I'm here,' said Mildred and looked very surprised. 'Moo,' she added.

'Well, I'm jiggered!' exclaimed Lord Spiffing. 'It worked! Well done, Norman – you won't regret it, I promise.' He gave his cow an affectionate pat on the nose. 'You're a wonder-cow, Mildred. Would you like a little treat for being so brave? You would? I'll fetch some of your delicious energy cakes from the shed.' And he set off towards a tiny, ramshackle hut near a clump of trees in the middle of the meadow.

Oli glanced at Mildred curiously and noticed a new glint in the cow's eye. Beyond her the meadow took on a rich golden glow and, turning round, Oli saw the western sky ablaze with fiery oranges and reds, seconds before the last flaming slice of sun was consumed by the black horizon.

Darkness now thickened all around, but when Oli turned back to Mildred he had a nasty shock. The glint in her eye, far from being snuffed out with the sun, had intensified to a burning gleam. Oli had a bad feeling about this.

'I think we should get back over the fence, fast,' he whispered to the others, with a nod in Mildred's direction. Skipjack followed the nod and his eyes widened. The little Jersey cow was growing bigger

and bigger, as if being inflated by an industrial pump.

'I think you're right,' he agreed.

'But what about Algy?' cried Lady Spiffing.

His Lordship had just emerged from the shed with a bucket and was pottering happily back through the dusky meadow.

Mildred by now had sprouted two sharp horns, a shaggy ridge of black hair and a long row of alarmingly sharp canine teeth. She turned round slowly to face her owner.

'Oh, no!' gasped Oli. 'This will be Norman's

revenge – to trample Lord Spiffing to bits!' He raised his voice and yelled, 'Run! She's a were-cow!'

'Where's the cow, did you say?' Lord Spiffing hollered back. 'Why, she's right there, in front of you!'

Oli turned to Skipjack. 'Stay here, and hold back Mildred,' he ordered and, without explaining just how his friend was supposed to hold back a 400-kilo were-cow hell-bent on revenge, he took off across the meadow.

His Lordship was ambling back towards his beloved Mildred at a gentle pace. He loved these early-autumn evenings. Here came that nice chap Oli to help him with the bucket. 'Slow down, my boy,' he called, but Oli grabbed the bucket and spun him round.

'It's Mildred,' the boy was gasping. 'Norman's turned her into a were-cow and she's after you.'

'Good grief!' In a state of utter shock, Lord Spiffing allowed himself to be hauled back to the shed and shoved inside.

Meanwhile Mildred's transformation from a doe-eyed pet into a steaming, stamping, black and bristling hunk of angry beef was almost complete and Skipjack was frantically trying to think of a way to hold her back. He considered using a rugby tackle but even his famous 'demolition ball', which had once forced no less a foe than Slugger Stubbins to bite the mud, wouldn't bring down this opponent.

Mildred began to snort and paw the ground.

'Ready or not . . .' muttered Norman.

Skipjack seized the cow's tail in both hands.

'Here I come!' Mildred shot off like big, hairy cannon ball. Skipjack held on valiantly but it was no good; he would have needed wings to keep up, or wheels. Just as he was vowing never again to get so close to a cow's bottom, he tripped on a tussock and came unhitched.

Losing her trailer gave Mildred extra thrust and Skipjack could have sworn she almost broke the land speed record as she made a bee-line for the shed in which Oli and Lord Spiffing had taken refuge.

'I'm afraid it's not a very sturdy shed,' whispered His Lordship listening anxiously to the thunder of approaching hoofs.

'Let's hope Mildred doesn't know that,' Oli

whispered back as the stampede screeched to a standstill a couple of feet away. 'Does it have a back door?' he asked without much hope; even castle sheds would only have one entrance. He was not surprised, therefore, when the reply was negative. But then Lord Spiffing added some welcome news.

'It does have a sort of back-gap,' he said. 'There's a bit of wall missing.'

The unmistakable voice of Norman at his very nastiest came whining through the woodwork.

'Little pig, little pig – let me come in!'

'Go away, Norman!' yelled Oli. 'A back-gap will do nicely,' he whispered to his cell-mate. 'You go first.'

'Does that mean,' enquired Norman, '"not by the hair of my chinny-chin-chin"?'

'No, it means go away, Norman,' replied Oli.

Lord Spiffing squeezed through the gap.

'Then I'll huff,' chuckled Norman wickedly.

Oli squeezed through the gap.

'And I'll puff,' continued Norman, who was clearly having the time of his life, or rather his death, 'and I'll blow your house down!'

The blow was a bit of a cheat, as it was helped

by a head-butt. But no ref was on hand to dish out a red card, and the feeble shack collapsed in a heap. By the time the dust had settled, its former inmates were sprinting towards the nearest fence.

For someone on the creaky side of sixty, His Lordship was astonishingly nippy. Even so, it was not long before hot bovine breath was on their backs and Oli knew that his team-mate would soon feel the sharp prod of horns and be tossed in the air like a salad tomato.

Suddenly, their pursuer jerked to a halt. Without pausing to find out why, Oli and Lord Spiffing hurled themselves at the fence and scrambled over to safety, while from somewhere behind them came a jubilant, 'Yee, ha!' Picking

themselves up and turning round, they saw that Mildred was now straining on a long stretch of rope, at the other end of which were three people. One was Skipjack, the second was Lady Spiffing and the third was Madam Moonbeam.

Oli, Lord Spiffing and Mildred all stared in disbelief as this amazing woman deftly tied the rope in great big knots around the nearest tree trunk. By the time the were-cow had recovered enough to think about punishing her three captors by steam-rolling them into the ground, they had legged it to safety.

'Fancy Madam Moonbeam being able to use a lasso,' said Oli in wonder as they rejoined the others.

'She is indeed – what's the word? Awesome,'

agreed Lord Spiffing.

Lady Spiffing came hurrying over to meet them. 'Algy!' she cried. 'Are you still in one piece?'

'Of course I am, Binky,' he said cheerfully. 'I haven't had so much fun for years.' He turned to Madam Moonbeam. 'How can I ever thank you, and where did you learn such a marvellous trick?'

She hesitated. '*Wild West Wagon Woman.* I'm afraid I've been deceiving you both. You see, I am not a real clairvoyant.'

Lady Spiffing waved a dismissive hand. 'Oh, I knew that,' she said.

Her husband looked baffled. 'Not real? And you knew, Binky? Since when?'

'Since the moment I saw her,' said Lady Spiffing.

'Was I that bad?' asked Madam Moonbeam sadly.

'Not at all – you were wonderful,' Lady Spiffing told her. 'But I saw you in a play once, many years ago, and you were wonderful in that, too. In fact, I never forgot it, so of course I recognised you straight away.'

Madam Moonbeam turned a modest shade of pink.

'In any case,' chuckled Lady Spiffing, 'Great-great-grandfather Gerald should have been short and fat.'

'Why didn't you tell me she was a phoney?' demanded her husband.

She shrugged. 'I didn't want to spoil the fun. Besides, it was all going so well – the visitors loved Gerald.'

'I suppose you won't need me any more, now that you've found the treasure,' said Madam Moonbeam in a small voice.

'My dear Madam Moonbeam,' said Lord Spiffing, 'we'd have to find a whole box of Golden Scarabs to set this old place straight. Until that happens we shall certainly need you. Someone has to rally up my dreadful departed for those nincompoop tourists.'

Tears welled up in the Moonbeam eyes and, as she stepped forward with outstretched arms, Lord Spiffing realised with great alarm that he was about to be hugged. His wife intervened hastily on his behalf.

'Why don't you start with the Blue Lady in the drawing room?' she suggested.

It worked: Madam Moonbeam forgot all about embracing Lord Spiffing and eagerly began to describe the puff of blue smoke.

She was interrupted by a terrible, bloodcurdling howl. Mildred the were-cow had given up glaring at them from the end of her rope and had trotted off to a distant hummock to bay at the moon. Lady Spiffing looked dismayed.

'I hope she doesn't keep that up all night – she'll upset the dogs.'

'It's good advertising though – I'll get my video camera,' said Madam Moonbeam and she bustled off happily.

Lord Spiffing gazed at the strange silhouette of his favourite cow and gave a deep sigh.

'She'll be fine in the morning,' said Oli comfortingly.

'And just think,' added Skipjack, 'it could have been you.'

* * *

Half an hour later the boys were upstairs packing when Oli glanced out of the window and happened to see his mother's car approaching the castle, with Daisy and Tara in the back. So when the boys came down the stairs and were assaulted by ghostly wails from behind the two suits of armour in the hall, they were not in the least bit surprised.

'Who shall we put on the right wing of our dream team?' asked Oli, extra loudly, as they passed.

'What about that really speedy Irish guy, O'thingy?' suggested Skipjack, equally loudly.

They arrived in the kitchen and had just said 'Hi' to Oli's mum when the girls burst in, breathless.

'Doesn't your caretaker ever stop sweeping the hall?' Tara demanded.

'Caretaker?' replied Lady Spiffing vaguely. 'Oh, have you seen Wilson? He sometimes appears to children. He doesn't like them at all.'

'Never did,' put in His Lordship. 'When I was a boy he used to follow us round, waiting for the chance to tick us off. Of course, now he can only stand there with his broom, frowning and shaking his head.'

The colour drained from Tara's face. 'You mean, the caretaker is . . . is . . .' she stammered.

'A ghost, dear? Yes, that's right.'

Tara and Daisy turned to face one another in horror and then ran away squealing into the yard.

Skipjack leaned across to Oli and whispered, 'I think you've won your bet.'

Note on Oli's pillow that night, beside a pot containing Triffid the Venus Fly Trap:

ALL RIGHT YOU WIN.

Letter sent to Spiffing Castle three days later on British Museum paper:

Dear Lord and Lady Spiffing,
I am delighted to report that the artefact known as 'The Golden Scarab of Pharoah Amenhotep III' is indeed genuine and that this museum would like to purchase it from you, as agreed. I enclose a cheque for half a million pounds.
Yours sincerely,
Anthony Tickwitty
Chief Egyptologist

Letter sent to Spiffing Castle three days later on a grubby sheet of lined A4:

Dear Lord and Lady Spiffing,
Thanks for an awesome weekend. We'll never forget Beetle or Norman. Skipjack's brother Matt has given up para-psychology and said we could keep the Spookoscope but we've kind of had enough of ghost-hunting for a while cos the rugby season's just started and we thought maybe Madam Moonbeam would like to have another go so here it is.
From
Oli and Skipjack

Letter sent back to the boys on Spiffing Castle writing paper:

Dear Oli and Skipjack,
We are the ones who must thank *you*. So much has changed here: the roof is being repaired and Madam Moonbeam is a wonder – we don't know how we managed without her. She and Uncle Beetle do a

marvellous routine for the tourists. He complains about being sucked up her nose every day but I think he secretly enjoys all the attention.

Cousin Norman is very happy with Mildred, who suffered no ill-effects from her night as a were-cow. Mildred is now a superstar and the tourists come flocking to see the famous haunted cow. Norman says that she is very clever and that the whole staring into space thing that cows do is just to get us to leave them in peace. He says if people had spent a million years standing about eating grass they might have had time to think interesting thoughts, too.

Come and visit us soon,

Lots of love,

Agatha Spiffing

MIRROR MISCHIEF COMING IN JAN 2010

MAGIC TROUBLE!

Maths teacher Vernon Surd punishes anyone who can't do fractions (= Oli).

School bully Slugger Stubbins punishes anyone who dodges his rugby tackles (= Oli).

But when Oli uses his new magic mirror to punish his punishers, they go absolutely WILD!

Now only Skipjack can save his friend, with a bit of help from the Zombie Witch Doctor . . .

ALSO AVAILABLE